THE TIMEKEEPERS

The Ancient Olympics

D1240036

Contents

Chapter 1

Adventure time

It was the final game of the soccer
tournament, so the crowd didn't mind
the hot Mexican sun. They shouted
and cheered as the clock counted down
the last seconds of the match. Rosa's
team was tied 2-2, and the ball
was in midfield.

"Come on, Rosa," she said to herself. "We can still win!"

She dodged the girl who was guarding her and raised an arm—she was open and onside. Her teammate kicked the ball across the goal, straight towards Rosa.

Suddenly, the ball stopped in mid-air and the players were as still as statues. The crowd of spectators were silent, their flags stopped in mid-wave.

There was no birdsong, no distant roar of traffic—not a sound.

Rosa wasn't worried—she knew exactly what was happening! Instead, she was excited. Rosa belonged to a secret organization called the Timekeepers, who could visit the past, putting history back on track when it had gone wrong. And a villain, named DeLay, was always causing chaos throughout the centuries…

Rosa glanced at her wrist. The hands on her special watch were spinning backward! She was being called to the History Hub, the Timekeepers' HQ.

DeLay must have messed up history again, she thought.

Rosa flipped up her watch face to reveal a screen of buttons, and pressed the biggest one. She gasped as her feet left the ground amid a whirl of colors. Brilliant white light hid the pitch, the stadium, everything…

The next moment, Rosa's soccer boots touched down and the white light shimmered and disappeared. She was inside a fantastic museum. Its shelves and glass-fronted display cabinets were crammed with historical objects. The History Hub!

"Rosa, here!" she called, then glanced at some of the objects: a young prince's crown from the 14th century, a papyrus scroll from Ancient Egypt, and a gold locket containing a piece of paper that was too fragile to unfold.

Something rustled. Rosa looked up at a large cuckoo clock on the wall. A little red door opened and a bright-eyed bird looked out.

"Cuckoo!" the bird said.

"Hi, Tempo!" said Rosa. "Am I first to arrive?"

"Cuckoo!" the bird replied, bobbing her head.

White light flashed and a dark-haired girl appeared. "Yasmin, here!" she said. Yasmin loved all things technology!

Flash!

"Kingsley, here," sang the next Timekeeper. He popped a guitar pick into the little box he kept in his pocket.

Flash!

Sarah arrived, clutching her notebook as usual. A chain around her neck held a little silver pen with a tiny blue gem on the end, like a drop of ink. "I was writing a poem," she said.

Rosa grinned. Sarah was always full of writing ideas.

Then came Hannah with a paintbrush, and a blob of red paint on her nose. She was followed by Jackson, who had flour on his hands and brought the delicious aroma of fresh bread. He loved baking!

Luke and Min-Jun appeared together. Luke wore a black jacket studded across the back with a row of stars, and a matching belt. He twirled. "Like my latest creation?" he asked.

"Yeah! I want that jacket!" said Kingsley.

"Cool belt," said Hannah. "And look at what Min-Jun's made!" she added. "Um, what is it, Min-Jun?"

"It's a truck for my model airport," he said. "Well, it will be when it's finished." He glanced at Rosa, who was in her soccer uniform. "Good game?"

"Brilliant," Rosa said. "We've still got a few seconds to go before the whistle." Time stayed still while the Timekeepers were away, so she knew she'd be back to

finish the game. Right now, she was
excited to discover what problem
was happening in the past, and who
would be having an adventure.

The Timekeepers gathered around an
empty glass display case. A ball of light
filled the case, then splintered into white
sparks. The sparks cleared to reveal a
small red and black jug with a stopper in
the top. The neck was long and narrow,
with a loop-shaped handle, and it was
decorated with running figures on one
side, and two wrestlers on the other.

"The pictures seem to tell a story," said Sarah. "A sporty story."

Jackson opened the display case and took out the tiny jug. He removed the stopper and sniffed. "It's olive oil," he said.

"The painting's in an ancient style," Hannah said thoughtfully. "I think this object must be an ancient Greek flask."

"I think you're right," said Rosa. "I've read that athletes used to oil their bodies before playing sport. Afterwards, they scraped off the oil, and the dirt and sweat came with it."

"DeLay must be causing trouble in Ancient Greece," said Min-Jun. His eyes sparkled. "So who's going back in time today?"

Tempo tilted her head as if she was thinking. She flew across the room and landed on Rosa's head. "Cuckoo!"

Rosa gasped. "It's me!" she cried. Her heart pounded and her knees felt weak.

"Lucky you!" said Min-Jun. "Don't forget, we'll be here if you need help."

Tempo circled the room, then swooped down onto Kingsley's shoulder. "Woo-hoo!" he cried, grinning at Rosa. "I'm coming, too!" They high-fived. "Ancient Greece is going to be quite a change from Nigeria," Kingsley added.

"And Mexico!" said Rosa. She took the little flask from Jackson. "This must be important to help us beat DeLay," she said, tucking it into her shorts pocket. "Though I can't imagine how olive oil will be useful..."

She and Kingsley stood together, and Tempo circled their heads.

"Cuckoo!" Faster and faster the bird flew until she was just a blur. They heard

a single clock chime, followed by a burst of bright white light…

As the light shimmered and disappeared, the first thing Rosa and Kingsley noticed was the hot sun.

The second thing was their clothes: they were now wearing white linen tunics with short cloaks and sandals, and Rosa had a cross-body bag holding the flask of olive oil.

The third thing was that they were in a long, narrow stadium. It seemed to have been dug out of the land, rather than built upon it. A sandy track ran the length of the arena. Circling the stadium were grassy banks for people to sit on, like giant steps. There were hundreds, or even thousands, of people sitting there, speaking excitedly. Rosa noticed a short row of stone seats, and guessed they were for important people.

"So this is Ancient Greece!" said Kingsley. "But where are we, exactly? And when are we?"

Rosa checked her watch. "This is Olympia, and it's the year 408 BCE."

"Wow!" said Kingsley. "We've gone back in time, nearly..." He did a quick calculation. "...Nearly 2,500 years!

A thrill shivered through Rosa. "If this is Olympia," she said, "and we're standing in a stadium...then we're at one of the Ancient Olympic Games!"

Chapter 2

Musical mix-up

Not long ago, Rosa had watched the Olympics on TV. Now she was here, in Ancient Greece, where the Olympic Games had begun!

It was hot in the sun, so Rosa was glad her long hair was tucked under a wide-brimmed hat. She realized lots of

the crowed were wearing similar hats —
through strangely, they were all men
and boys. She couldn't see any
women or girls at all.

Tempo liked the hat, too. She perched
on Rosa's shoulder, in the shade of
the brim.

"Kingsley, I think I should pretend
I'm a boy," Rosa said. "The History Hub
has dressed me like one, and it always
gets that kind of thing right."

He nodded. "There'll be a reason."

"Koo!" said Tempo, bobbing her head.

"See? She agrees," said Kingsley.

Rosa laughed, and looked around. "No sign of DeLay," she said. "Let's join the crowd and and see if we can spot any clues about where he might be."

They threaded through the crowd of men and boys, and sat down in a space on one of the grassy steps, looking down at the track. Tempo tucked herself into Rosa's bag, next to the olive oil.

In the center of the stadium, a parade of important-looking people dressed in colorful robes were making their way to a large, shallow bowl, which contained burning logs. Rosa gasped. She nudged Kingsley and pointed to it.

"The Olympic flame! We still have one today, as a link to the Ancient Games," she whispered. "It's amazing seeing one of the originals!"

A large group of men and boys was standing near the fire bowl. They weren't wearing many clothes—most just wore short skirts, a bit like kilts, and many were barefoot. Rosa guessed that they were athletes.

Kingsley nodded. "They're nothing like modern competitors, are they?" he said. "No sportswear or sneakers."

"Let's begin, priest," called a tall man with a curly beard, who was standing beside the fire bowl.

The priest stepped forward, his long yellow robe swirling around him. The crowd stopped speaking, and leaned forward to listen.

"In the name of the great god Zeus," the priest announced, "let this new day of the 93rd Olympic Games begin. Athletes, remember the oath you swore before Zeus, that you will compete with honor."

"He must mean, no cheating," whispered Kingsley.

The priest continued. "Remember the Ekecheiria—the sacred Olympic truce. You are from different city states, and some of you are at war with each other. There must be no fighting for the three months of the Truce, so all may travel safely to and from the Games."

There was some mumbling in the crowd. Rosa noticed two men beside the fire bowl glaring at each other. "I bet they're from warring states," she said to Kingsley.

"By Zeus, I should say so!" said a tall, blond boy, who was sitting on the other side of Rosa. "That's the Prince of Sparta with the big helmet, and the one with the blue tunic is the Prince of Athens. I thought everyone knew that." He looked curiously at the Timekeepers. "Where are you from, then?"

"Um…a land far from here," said Rosa. "We're travelers. This is Kingsley, and I'm, umm…Ross," she said, using the first boy's name she could think of that sounded like Rosa.

"Unusual names. But you're Greek, aren't you?" said the boy. He laughed.

"You must be or you wouldn't be here. No foreigners are allowed! I'm a Rhapsode," he continued. "I've walked all the way here from my home in Athens to recite poetry. I'm going to be famous. Karpos is the *name*—poetry's my *game*!"

"Is performing poetry a Rhapsode's job?" asked Rosa.

Karpos's eyes widened. "You don't know much, do you? Yes, I write it, too," he said. "Don't you have Rhapsodes back home?"

"We have performance poets," said Kingsley, "only they're not called Rhapsodes."

"What a strange place you must be from," said Karpos.

"Cuckoo!" said Tempo, poking her head out of Rosa's bag.

"Hello little bird," said Karpos, offering her one of the figs he was snacking on. Tempo ate it up.
"Is it yours?"

"Tempo doesn't belong to anybody," said Kingsley, "but she loves spending, umm... time... with us."

Musicians at the side of the arena started playing. Kingsley recognised some of their instruments from a history project at school, and pointed them out to Rosa. "Those are drums, they're lyres—the ones like little harps—and that noisy one is a horn..."

But something was wrong.

"By Apollo's ears!" Karpos said, clapping his hands over his own ears. "Those musicians are terrible. **Boom boom bang—hoot toot twang**!"

Rosa laughed and whispered to Kingsley, "They are awful, aren't they? What a mix-up! But why are they making such a terrible noise?"

Kingsley listened carefully. "It sounds like they're playing the right music," he said, "but some of them are too fast, and some of them are too slow. They're all out of time."

Rosa gasped. *Out of time!*

"This must mean that DeLay's somewhere around here," Rosa said nervously. DeLay had a way of messing about with time for a few moments. He would throw a Time Crunch, a special device he invented that helps him briefly control the flow of time.

"Let's find out what he's doing," Rosa said.

The Timekeepers made their way through the crowd, climbing down the grassy steps, toward the musicians. Meanwhile, the athletes were warming up, running on the spot and stretching, just like Rosa did before a game. As they got close to the musicians, Kingsley pointed to a man sneaking along the edge of the arena. "Is that DeLay?"

The man wore a knee-length tunic with a clock design on it. A leather pouch hung from his belt, and the sandals on his bony feet turned up at the toes. Rosa thought they looked as though they were snarling. The figure stooped, as if he didn't want to be noticed. But there was no mistaking the pale straw-coloured hair. "It's DeLay alright," Rosa said grimly. "Let's stop him before he causes chaos!"

Chapter 3

The feud

The day's events were beginning. As Rosa and Kingsley followed DeLay through the stadium, athletes were training hard and people were selling snacks to the excited crowd. The scent of mint and honey wafted around. "Get your olives here!" yelled one. "Olives so tasty, they're fit for a feast at Mount Olympus!"

"That's the home of their gods and goddesses," said Rosa, remembering what she'd learned about ancient Greece at school.

They were passing the big stone blocks that separated the seating area from the stadium. These were surrounded by a ditch filled with running water. Tempo dipped her beak into it for a quick drink, then flapped out of the way of the athletes who were gathering beside it. They wore helmets and metal armor, and each carried a huge shield. Rosa tried to imagine what modern athletes would think of those outfits!

Officials now waited by the starting

line, and the watching crowd were telling each other excitedly, "It's time for the Hoplite race!"

"A hopping race?" Kingsley said in amazement.

"Nice joke!" It was Karpos again, holding a big bowl of olives that he'd bought. "Oh," he said, "you really don't know? It's called that because the athletes are armored like a kind of soldier called a Hoplite."

Rosa and Kingsley watched, amazed, as the athletes headed for the start line. "Those shields must be so heavy," Rosa said. "The race will be a test of strength as well as speed."

Kingsley pointed to two competitors

striding to the start. "There are the Prince of Sparta and the Prince of Athens," he said. "Do princes run in races, Karpos?"

"Of course they do," Karpos said, chewing on an olive. "A prince who sprints is a prince who…glints? Hints? Hold on, a rhyme will come to me…"

At the other end of the arena,

DeLay was heading up an aisle
between the rows of spectators.

"Sorry, Karpos," said Rosa.
"Got to go!"

Rosa and Kingsley ran up the next

aisle. They kept looking across at DeLay, trying to draw level with the fleeing villain. Running up steep steps was easy for his long, skinny legs, but as the Timekeepers reached the top level, they were exhausted. "I feel like I've run a marathon," gasped Kingsley.

DeLay put a thumb to his nose and waved his fingers at the Timekeepers. "Can't catch me!" he jeered, and headed back down the aisle.

Kingsley and Rosa sighed.

A trumpet blast echoed through the arena. The Hoplite race was beginning!

Rosa could hardly believe how fast the competitors could run in their armor. As she and Kingsley ran back down the steps, the runners passed right by, kicking up big clouds of dust.

The crowd cheered and shouted.

DeLay reached the arena, and dived
into the dust clouds.

"Oh no, he's using the dust as cover to
get away," Rosa said. "We've lost him!"

The crowd roared. The race was
finishing. "The princes are neck and
neck," said Kingsley. "Sparta's edging
forward… Athens is gaining on him…
Sparta wins!"

The Spartan spectators cheered wildly

and the Athenians booed. The Spartan
prince punched a hand to the sky
in victory.

Tempo flew around Rosa's shoulder
and dropped a twig into her hand. It had
two plump, purple plums dangling from
it. "Cuckoo-oo-oo,"
she said.

"Thank you," said Rosa, stroking

Tempo's wing feathers. "That's cheered me up about losing DeLay."

"Me too," Kingsley said, as he pulled a plum from the twig. "I hope you had one too, Tempo."

She bobbed her head. "Cuckoo!"

The officials they had seen by the fire bowl were making their way to a podium. "I think they're about to give out the awards," said Rosa. "Keep an eye out for DeLay!"

The podium was close to Rosa and Kingsley. As the priest passed by, Rosa smelled a familiar scent. It was a bit like rosemary, which was a herb her mum added to some of her favorite meals.

"It is my honor to present the winner's prize," the priest said.

A servant carrying a dark red cushion stepped forward. Instead of medals, a ribbon lay on it, beside a wreath of leaves. The priest tied the ribbon around the Prince of Sparta's head.

"This marks the winner as an

Olympic champion," the priest said.
"The wreath is made from olive branches
cut from the sacred tree behind the
Temple of Zeus. It will remain in the
temple until the final day of the Games,
when all champions will be crowned
with wreaths."

As the servant turned away, Rosa
noticed something strange. He was
moving as slowly as a sleepy tortoise. The
priest's robes were billowing slowly too,
and the Prince of Sparta's grin seemed to

spreading very, very slowly across his face... too slowly...

The Timekeepers looked at each other. "Time Crunch," they said together.

Rosa blinked. Just as suddenly as time had slowed down, it returned to normal.

The servant stared at his empty cushion. "The wreath!" he yelled. "It's gone!"

What a stink

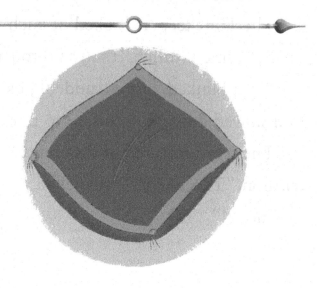

The Spartan Prince marched furiously over to the Prince of Athens. "You're behind this!" he snapped.

The Athenian prince said sharply, "I would never steal."

The Prince of Sparta whirled round to the officials. "He either stole my crown,

or got someone else to do it!
What else could have happened?"

A brief fight broke out and the crowd
was in uproar. Groups of Spartans shook
their fists at the Athenians, and it seemed
as if everyone was yelling.

"Athenians are cheats!"

"Spartans are liars!"

Only the Timekeepers knew what was really going on. "DeLay's the thief," Rosa said grimly. "He's used a Time Crunch to steal the wreath—and look at the chaos it's causing!"

Tempo was sitting on Rosa's shoulder, covering her head with her wings.

"She doesn't like the noise," said Kingsley. "It's OK, Tempo."

"By all the gods, it was NOT me!" roared the Prince of Athens. Tempo was so startled that she flew off, squawking.

"Look!" cried the Spartan Prince. "That bird! It is a bad omen! There is thievery and cheating at these Games!"

Kingsley watched Tempo in alarm as she flew out of the arena, the crowd gaping and pointing at her. "I hope she's okay."

"She's a clever bird," Rosa said. "She'll be back when things calm down. In the meantime, if we can find that wreath, the Spartans and Athenians will stop arguing. If we can't, and if a fight breaks out, the Olympic Truce will be broken. There could be a war."

Kingsley nodded. "And if the city states can't trust each other to compete fairly—well, there might never be another Olympic Games!"

"What a terrible thought," said Rosa, with a shudder. The Olympics were where the best athletes competed against each other, but she knew it had also become one of the greatest expressions of cooperation and common values among the nations of the world.

Kingsley noticed that the priest had taken the angry princes aside. "He's trying to make peace—" He stopped. Rosa was staring towards the athletes' tunnel entrance.

"Hello? Earth to Rosa?" said Kingsley.

"Sorry! I'm sure I saw DeLay," she said. "Look there…"

The villain was slinking into the tunnel.

"He's leaving the stadium," said Kingsley.

They ran across the arena. No one stopped them—everyone was either too busy arguing, or too busy watching the princes, who were standing opposite each other now, both red with fury. The priest had his hands out, trying to keep them apart.

As the Timekeepers entered the tunnel, DeLay glanced back and spotted them.

"Bye, losers!" he shouted as he vanished through the exit.

"After him!" cried Rosa.

They sprinted through the tunnel, and found themselves almost on the edge of the vast Olympic campground. Thousands of tents stretched as far as they could see. Some were tall and brightly coloured, and big enough to hold a party in. Others were just blankets propped up with sticks. People were cooking on fires, chatting, laughing, and playing games.

"This isn't how I imagined ancient Greece," said Kingsley. "I expected white buildings and groves of almond and olive trees. And people sitting in the shade eating olives and discussing maths, philosophy, and poetry."

"Me too," Rosa said. "Look, if we cut across the corner of the campsite we'll get to the Olympic buildings. I know there's a temple and a hippodrome—"

Kingsley gasped. "They have *hippos*?"

Rosa laughed as they wound their way between the tents. "No, hippos is the Greek word for horse. The hippodrome's for horse races."

"How come you know that?" Kingsley asked.

"I learned a few Greek words when I did a school project on ancient Greece," said Rosa. "I also learned that the hippodrome's not just for horse racing. It's for chariot racing, too."

"Chariots!" said Kingsley. "Amazing!"

Tempo flew down to meet them, with two berries in her beak.

"Glad you're OK, Tempo," said Kingsley.

"This snack delivery service is excellent!"

"Cuckoo!" Tempo fluffed her feathers, looking pleased with herself.

Rosa spotted a familiar figure nearby. It was Karpos the Rhapsode, and he looked confused. She called to him. "What's wrong, Karpos?"

"I can't find my tent, and I don't know which way to turn," he said. "Is it left or is it right? One thing's sure, it's out of *sight*!"

Kingsley was wrinkling his nose. "Ugh!" he said. "What's that stink?"

Karpos laughed. "It's the smell of thousands of people who've got nowhere to wash and nowhere to go to the toilet."

"Whaaat?" said Kingsley. "What do you mean, nowhere to go to the toilet?"

"If we need to go, we dig a hole, or find a stream," said Karpos.

"Pollution alert!" said Kingsley. Rosa laughed.

Karpos gave a shout and waved a hand toward a tattered brown tent. "Thank Athena, there it is! I'm off to get my lyre. See you."

Rosa and Kingsley hurried on, looking all around them for DeLay. A woman carrying a basket of cooked fish pushed past. "Sardines!" she called. "Fresh from the Mediterranean!" There were lots of other food and trinket sellers too. A man with a stall that had little plumes of smoke swirling from it shouted, "Get your lovely incense here! Burn my amazing incense and Zeus will hear your prayers!" He took some coins from a customer. "Thanks," he said, passing the customer a small bottle. "Made from the best frankincense your money can buy."

The incense blew around Rosa and Kingsley passed him. It was a strong, rosemary scent. Rosa remembered the priest smelling like that too. "They must use frankincense in their temples," she said. "It's much nicer than the smells around here."

Tempo flapped her wings.

"*Cuck-koo-koo-koo*," she squawked, and flew off again.

"Now where's she gone?" wondered Kingsley.

"Probably looking for more snacks," said Rosa.

A line of horse-drawn chariots were waiting to enter a huge stadium. The brightly-painted chariots looked rather like fancy carts with no back, and each was pulled by two horses.

"Chariots! So that stadium must be the hippodrome," said Kingsley. "There's probably a race starting soon. I know we need to find DeLay, but shall we go and see? Just quickly?"

Rosa nodded. Everything was so exciting, it was hard to resist! They crossed the busy camp as fast as possible without stepping on someone sleeping in the sunshine, treading in leftover food or burning their feet on a campfire.

"I wonder why some of the chariots have two drivers," said Kingsley.

A man watching the chariots leaned in and said, "Not two drivers, boy. One's the owner. It's the owner who gets the glory, without any of the danger."

"Is it very dangerous?" asked Rosa.

The man spat out pomegranate seeds and laughed. "Chariot-racing's probably the most dangerous sport in the Olympic Games," he said.

Rosa pointed. "There! DeLay is heading for the chariots!"

DeLay turned the corner and headed straight toward the line of chariots. He leaped into the front one, pushed the driver out, and grabbed the reins!

The last thing the Timekeepers
saw was DeLay's sneering face as
he and his chariot disappeared into
the hippodrome.

Kingsley looked at Rosa in dismay.
"He's going to ruin another event!"

Rosa shook her head. "Not if we
stop him…"

Chapter 5

Chariot race

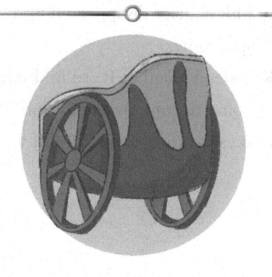

As the chariots rumbled into the stadium, Rosa noticed one that hadn't joined the line. It had no driver, just a woman in a long, tunic dress and a cloak, who was holding the reins. She glanced around impatiently, as if she was searching for someone. A second woman stood nearby.

As they neared the pair, Rosa heard the woman holding the reins say, "Where is he, Irene? We've come all this way. What else can I do?"

"Nothing, Alkistis," Irene said soothingly. "You can't drive the chariot yourself. Without your driver, your chariot's out of the race. We won't be able to enter this year."

"I wish I *could* drive it," said Alkistis. "They're my horses, it's my chariot, and I'm a good driver. It's only because I'm a woman that I'm not allowed. It's not fair."

"Maybe things will be different one day," Irene said.

An idea flashed through Rosa. She grabbed Kingsley's elbow. "We could drive her chariot," she said. "Everyone thinks I'm a boy. That way we'll keep DeLay in our sights *and* help Alkistis."

"You're kidding," Kingsley said. "We've never done anything like that in our lives!"

"Well, I used to drive my aunt's pony cart," said Rosa. "It can't be that different. Can it?"

"It's an Olympic race!" Kingsley exclaimed, but Rosa pulled him over to Alkistis, who was turning the chariot around. "Stop!" Rosa cried.

The women stared. "Can I help you, young man?" said Alkistis.

"I want to help you," said Rosa. "My friend and I will race your chariot. If you'll let us."

Both women's eyes widened in surprise. "You're very young and very brave," said Irene, "but—"

"Please let us," Kingsley interrupted.

Alkistis grinned. "Why not?" She handed Rosa the reins.

Kingsley jumped into the chariot and pulled Rosa in after him. "Whatever you do, don't let your hat blow off and show your long hair!" he whispered.

"OK. Let's do this!" Rosa clicked her tongue and shook the reins. She felt the same mix of focus and excitement she had before a big soccer game.

"Good luck!" called Alkistis and Irene, as the chariot rumbled away.

Rosa tweaked the reins, guiding their two horses to follow the other chariots into the hippodrome. It was much bigger than the stadium they had already seen, and it was packed with noisy, excited spectators. At the far end was a post that the drivers had to go around before coming back down the other side of the oval track.

An official waved their chariot forward to the start line and Kingsley climbed in.

Don't pull the reins when you want to stop, Rosa kept telling herself. She remembered her aunt saying that if she did that, her pony would go faster. Would it be the same for chariot-horses? *Why am I worrying about stopping?* she thought. *We haven't started yet!*

There were about six chariots at the start line. Rosa felt a twinge of fear. She swallowed hard. She'd seen a chariot race in a movie, and she knew that crashes happened all the time. Here she was, in the midst of a closely packed row of snorting horses, who stamped and pawed the ground. She could almost feel the danger. The chariot rocked as if it, too, was anxious to start.

"Can you see DeLay, Kingsley?"
she asked.

"He's six chariots along the line," he
said. "An official's getting ready to blow
his horn. I think we're about to go." He
gripped the front of the chariot hard.

The crowd roared. Rosa's heart
seemed to jump into her mouth.

The horn blasted. They were off!

Rosa's horses must have done this dozens of times before. They leaped forward without her doing anything more than holding on to the reins.

And they were fast! There were only a few chariots in front of them, and DeLay was in one of them!

The chariots thundered around the oval track. The sound of wheels and hooves was deafening. There were screams when DeLay's chariot drove into another, forcing it off the track.

"He's playing dirty!" yelled Kingsley. "Watch out—we're coming up to the post! Don't turn too sharply!"

The chariot in front of them overshot, and tipped over. The driver ran for cover, while his horses carried on pulling the empty chariot. Her heart thumping, Rosa tugged the reins gently, guiding their horses safely round.

Now they were cantering down a straight section of the track. Rosa flicked the reins, urging the horses to go faster. DeLay's chariot was just ahead!

They drew alongside him, the horses' hooves pounding the track. DeLay spotted them, and a crooked smile spread across his face. He reached down into the chariot, and pulled up a tree branch.

Rosa's stomach turned over as she guessed what DeLay was up to. She tugged the reins, trying to turn the horses away, but it was too late—DeLay leaned over to their chariot, and jammed the wood into the spokes of their wheel.

The chariot tipped sideways and slid along. DeLay had knocked the wheel off! It rolled away, toward the roaring crowd.

"Hold on!" Kingsley yelled. Rosa was thrown against Kingsley. Their horses hadn't slowed down, and they were boxed in by dozens of thundering hooves and wheels.

They were about to be trampled!

Chapter 6

Catch DeLay

Think! Rosa told herself desperately. She and Kingsley couldn't hold on for much longer—soon they would tumble out among the clattering wheels and pounding hooves. She knew they had only one chance.

"Hurry, Kingsley! Your watch!" she shrieked above the noise. "Freeze!"

Kingsley flipped up his watch face and pressed a button.

Time froze.

Immediately, their horses were like sculptures in mid-gallop. Their chariot had tilted to rest on its axel—a long, strong piece of wood that usually had two wheels fixed to it. Now it had just one.

Rosa glanced around the hippodrome. The crowd stood like statues with wide yelling mouths. Horses' manes and tails were frozen in flight.

Rosa and Kingsley scrambled to their feet, brushing sand from their hands and faces.

"Wow," said Kingsley, looking around.

"I've never done a Freeze before."

"Me neither," Rosa said.

The Timekeepers could only freeze time once on each mission, and it only lasted a short while. Freezes were risky—if they weren't careful, they could accidentally cause snags in history. They were strictly for emergency use only.

Apart from the Timekeepers, there was only one other flash of movement—a speck in the sky that grew larger and larger. Tempo!

She flew to Rosa's shoulder and nuzzled her cheek with a soft wing. "Cuckoo!"

"She's glad we're okay," said Kingsley. His head snapped around as he heard a movement.

Footsteps crunched on the track.

DeLay! "Nice trick," he called to them. "Shame it doesn't work on me!"

Rosa and Kingsley groaned. DeLay reached into his pouch for a Time Crunch and flung it at his horses.

Tick tick tick…

It exploded into a cloud of smoke. To Rosa's dismay, DeLay's horses began moving. They weren't galloping at normal speed – they looked like a video being played in slow motion. But still, Rosa knew DeLay might get away before she and Kingsley could climb through the other chariots and catch him.

"Ha!" DeLay was cackling as he drove his chariot, very slowly but surely, along the track. "Give up, Timekeepers. You've lost. You'll never get the wreath back…and these are the last Olympic Games anyone will ever see!"

"We need help," Rosa decided. She pressed a button on her watch. Instantly, the other six Timekeepers appeared on screen, as a gallery of faces.

"We're in trouble," said Rosa. Quickly, she explained the situation to their friends at the History Hub. "If we're going to catch DeLay, we must fix our wheel. Any ideas?"

"Does your chariot have

a toolbox?" asked Min-Jun.

Kingsley said no, but Rosa had noticed something tucked inside it. "We do have some spare pieces of harness for the horses," she said. "Some straps with buckles on them."

"Great!" said Yasmin. She loved tech, and was good at solving practical problems. "Put the wheel back on, just the same as the one on the other side. Then wrap a leather strap tightly around the end of the axel and buckle it."

"Got it," said Kingsley, already scrambling around for the straps.

"That should hold the wheel on long enough for you to catch DeLay," said Yasmin.

"Thanks!" Kingsley and Rosa said.

Six voices cried,
"Good luck!" as the
call ended.

Rosa sprinted
towards the rows of
frozen faces to get the
runaway wheel. She rolled it back. The
empty chariot was quite light, so she and
Kingsley lifted it easily and slid the wheel
into place. Rosa wound a leather strap
around and around the end. She found
that once she'd buckled it, it felt
really solid.

"Just in time," said Kingsley.
"The Freeze is ending!"

Their horses gave a snort. The crowd
cheered. And the chariots began to speed
along the track once more.

Rosa let other chariots pass them. DeLay had escaped the crush and was heading for the exit at full gallop.

"After him!" cried Kingsley.

Sorry, Alkistis, Rosa thought. *We've broken your chariot, and now we're going to abandon the race. But we have to, to save the Olympics…*

Rosa spotted a gap between two chariots and drove straight through it.

DeLay glanced back. He turned purple with rage as he realized the Timekeepers were catching him up. He took another Time Crunch from his pouch and flung it back over his shoulder.

"Look out!" cried Kingsley. But it was a sloppy throw, and Rosa easily steered around the explosion of smoke.

Rosa and Kingsley kept going, steadily making ground and catching up with DeLay's chariot.

"What next?" said Kingsley as their chariot hurtled along.

"Get alongside him," said Rosa, giving him the reins. "I've got an idea, but it's risky!"

Once Kingsley got a clear run he drew level with DeLay.

"Okay," Rosa cried. "Here... I... GO!"

She leaped, just like a goalie jumping to make a save. She slammed into DeLay, just glimpsing his shocked face before he tumbled out of the back of the chariot. His horses halted, whinnying and tossing their manes.

"Whoa!" she heard Kingsley call to their own horses, stopping the chariot.

Rosa rummaged through DeLay's chariot. But apart from his cloak, there was nothing. "The wreath isn't here!" she said in dismay.

Kingsley ran over to them.
Rosa hopped down from DeLay's
chariot. DeLay lay on his back, getting
his breath back after his fall.
He glared up at them.

"Where's the wreath?"
Rosa demanded.

DeLay sniggered, but his eyes
were cold.

Kingsley was furious. "Where is it?"

"I've hidden it," DeLay sneered.

Chapter 7

Where's that wreath?

DeLay rolled away from the Timekeepers and leaped up. He sprinted off, looking like a speeding ostrich.

"Catch him!" Kingsley cried.

Rosa and Kingsley gave chase, but the tricky villain was too fast. After a few minutes of dashing around the fig trees, they could tell it was hopeless.

"He hasn't got the wreath anyway," Rosa said. "We need a new plan…"

She frowned as she jogged to a stop. A familiar, rosemary-like smell wafted back from DeLay. Incense, she thought. She'd smelled it on the priest, and on the stallholder.

"Maybe DeLay's been in a temple," said Rosa. "Could that be where he hid the wreath?"

They unharnessed both sets of horses form the chariots, and left them with some others who were eating oats from a trough. Then they headed back across the Olympic grounds, taking a short cut through an arch into a wide grass rectangle, surrounded by low buildings. A sign said: "Gymnasium". Lots of athletes wearing loincloths were practising their sports.

As they exited the gymnasium, a young woman in a short tunic jogged towards them.

"I wonder why she's here?" said Rosa. "We know now women weren't allowed in the Ancient Olympics. Excuse me," she called. "Are you an athlete?"

"Yes. I'm training for the Heraean Games. They take place after the Olympic Games," she said.

"We're from a faraway land," said Kingsley, "so we don't know much about your customs. Are the Heraean Games for women?"

The young woman nodded. "They're in honor of Hera, Queen of the Gods, and wife of Zeus," she said. "Only girls and women are allowed at our games. We're training close by—come and see."

"I wish we could," Rosa said. She'd love to see the women training, but finding the victor's wreath was much more important. "But we have to go to a temple."

"The temples are past our training ground. I'll show you," said the young woman. "I'm Melissa."

Rosa smiled. "This is Kingsley, and I'm, um, Ross. One of my best friends is called Melissa, too," she added. *Wow!* she thought. *That name's 2,000 years old!*

Melissa showed them a group of girls and women playing a ball game, sometimes throwing the ball, sometimes kicking it.

"Chrysanthe," Melissa called, "these visitors are from far away."

A girl ran over to say hello. "We're playing Episkyros," she said. "You throw or kick the ball, and try to get it past the other team, over the back line. It keeps us in shape!"

"In our land we play soccer," said Rosa, "but we can't use our hands."

Rosa asked, "Chrysanthe, has anyone odd been lurking about? He's skinny, with strange hair..."

"And a mean face..." added Kingsley.

"...And he's rude to people," Rosa finished.

"By Artemis, I know just who you mean!" said Chrysanthe. "He passed me as I ran through the olive grove, beneath the Hill of Kronos. There." She pointed to a cone-shaped peak, overlooking the Olympic grounds. "He shouted at me to get out of his way."

A ball from the Episkyros game bounced toward them. Without thinking, Rosa intercepted it, controlled it with her

chest then kicked it
back towards the players.

"Good kick!" Chrysanthe
and Melissa cried.

Rosa was thrilled. If only
she had time to stay and play.
*But I'd need my cleats, she thought,
instead of sandals!*

Rosa and Kingsley split up to search
the olive grove Chrysanthe had shown
them. "DeLay could easily have hidden
the wreath here," said Rosa. "Where
better to hide a wreath made of olive
leaves, but in an olive tree?"

A big sigh erupted from behind one
of the olive trees. Rosa and Kingsley
looked behind it. Sitting against the
trunk, his head in his hands, was Karpos.

A lyre was at his feet.

Rosa knelt down. "What's wrong?"

Karpos sighed again. "I'm feeling *bad*. I'm very *sad*."

"Why?" Rosa asked.

"Olympic champions have odes composed about their victories," he replied. "Poetry's my job, but… I'm stuck."

"Can we help?" asked Kingsley.

Karpos frowned. "I'm trying to think of something that rhymes with the Prince of Sparta's name."

"I write song lyrics," said Kingsley. "I'm sure I can help come up with a rhyme. What's the prince's name?"

"Agesipolis," said Karpos.

Rosa smothered a grin. Kingsley

gaped at Karpos. "You're trying to rhyme
with Agipo– Agipopol –Agipopolop –?"

Karpos nodded.

"Um," said Kingsley. "How about,
'Your sandals that are toeless? Your
enemies you demolish? Your armor you
do polish?' Ooh!" he said. "What about
rhyming with Sparta? 'Smarter, starter—
faster', but those aren't very
good rhymes."

"It doesn't have to rhyme exactly,"
said Karpos. "When I recite, I'll make it
sound right."

"Can we do this later?" asked Rosa.
"We think the prince's stolen wreath is in
a temple. Will you help us look?"

Karpos brightened up. "Friends from
faraway, helping you will make my *day*."

"Don't forget your lyre," said Kingsley.

Back at the Olympic complex, Karpos led them to a magnificent building, with great columns supporting the roof on every side. "This is the Temple of Zeus," he said. "You're lucky there's no line. People start gathering before dawn to make their offerings."

It was cool inside, and it took a minute for the Timekeepers' eyes to adjust to the dim light. The scent of frankincense swirled around them. There were a few people in there, but what caught their attention was an enormous statue of Zeus. It was made of ivory and gold and towered high above them.

Karpos whispered, "Even though he's seated on his throne, the statue towers over us."

"If Zeus could stand, he'd go through the roof!" said Kingsley delightedly. "Isn't it awesome?" he asked Rosa.

Awesome was exactly the word, Rosa thought. In fact, she knew the statue was considered one of the Seven Wonders of the Ancient World.

Karpos nudged Rosa. "Go on, make your offering. You shouldn't go any further until you do."

Her heart sank. "Karpos," she said, "we don't know your customs."

"I'll show you," he said. "What can you offer? Wine or oil would be good. Do you have any?"

Rosa's eyes shone. She opened her bag and took out the little flask.

Kingsley smiled. "So this is why the History Hub gave us the olive oil!"

Karpos showed Rosa a large bowl near the entrance. She removed the flask's stopper, bowed her head, and poured the oil into the bowl.

Suddenly, Tempo swooped down and dropped her own offering into the bowl—a large berry.

"Hello, friend," said Rosa, as Tempo hopped onto her shoulder. "I love berries.

It's cool how the ancient Greeks eat my favourite fruit!"

Now they had made their offerings, they made their way toward the statue.

"It's even more awesome up close," Rosa breathed. Zeus wore a gold robe and gold sandals, and a golden wreath on his head. A statuette of a winged woman stood on his hand.

"That's Nike," said Karpos. "She's the goddess of victory, but I'm sure you already knew that."

"Umm, yes," said Rosa, thinking, *Well, I do now!*

Kingsley leaned back to look up at Zeus's face. "What—?" he muttered, leaning a bit further back still. He almost bumped into Karpos, just behind him.

"What's up?" Rosa asked.

Kingsley whispered, "There are green leaves in Zeus's gold wreath! The stolen one is tucked into it."

Rosa's grinned with delight. "Great! It's a long way up, though. How are we going to get it down?

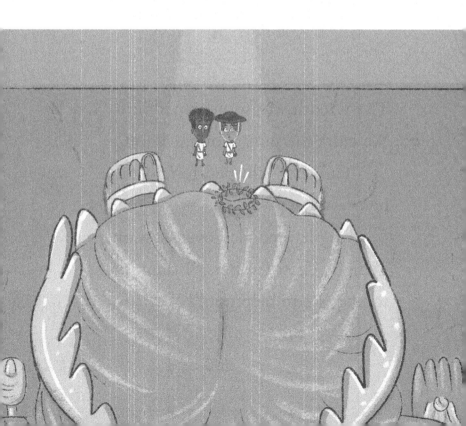

Chapter 8

Victory

The wreath was so near, yet out of reach.
We can't fail now, thought Rosa.

"Cuckoo!" chirped Tempo, on
her shoulder.

Kingsley reached over to stroke
Tempo's chest feathers. "I think she's
saying, 'I can help you!'"

"Cuckoo!" Tempo looked up at Zeus's head.

"She's offering to fly up and get the wreath!" Rosa said. Then something struck her. "Wait, Tempo." She glanced around. "Remember how the Spartan prince called her a bad omen? We don't want to worry everyone here. We need a distraction."

Kingsley grinned, and called to Karpos.

"Are you ready to perform your ode?" he asked.

"I can't wait," said Karpos. "It's ready now, thanks to your help with the rhymes. But someone normally plays my lyre as I recite."

"Kingsley will play it," said Rosa. "He's a great musician."

"I've never played a lyre," said Kingsley. "But I'd love to try."

The boys stood by the temple doorway. Kingsley strummed the lyre, just like a guitar, and Karpos began to recite.

"When at Olympia a prince did race,

Wowing the crowd with his impressive pace..."

The people from the temple were listening in silence. *They're spellbound by the performance,* thought Rosa. *Now's the time!*

"Go quickly, Tempo," she said. "No cuckooing!"

The bird flapped upward, disappeared from sight for a moment, then reappeared with the wreath in her beak. She dropped it into Rosa's waiting hands and fluttered to her shoulder.

"Thanks, Tempo," said Rosa, grinning at her friend.

"I knew that bird was a good omen," said a voice behind her. Rosa's heart flipped. She smelled the familiar scent of incense…

Turning around, she expected to see DeLay. But it was the priest, in his yellow robes.

It was the priest!

Rosa held out the wreath. "This is the one that was stolen," she said.

Applause broke out. The boys had finished. Kingsley bowed to the audience and hurried over to join them.

"As you found it, I think you should be the ones to carry it back where it belongs," the priest said. He smiled. "Mysterious strangers, Zeus must have sent you here to bring peace back to the Olympic Games. Follow me!"

As they left the temple, Rosa and Kingsley waved goodbye to Karpos. He was happily taking requests from his audience, and waved back.

"I've thought of an ode," Kingsley whispered to Rosa.

"Tell me," she said.

Kingsley began:

"My little rhyme

Tells how Keepers of Time

Saved an olive leaf crown

By bringing it down–"

"Cuck-OOO!" squawked Tempo.

"She's right," Rosa laughed. "We didn't bring the wreath down, she did!"

"I know," said Kingsley. "But you try finding a rhyme for 'cuckoo' or 'Tempo'. It's almost as hard as 'Agesipolis'."

Rosa laughed. "Good point!"

Back in the stadium, the priest stood between the Prince of Sparta and the Prince of Athens. "The Athenians didn't steal the wreath," he announced to the spectators. "Neither did the Spartans.

Perhaps Zeus took it because he was tired of the arguing."

He pointed to Kingsley and Rosa, who were close by. Rosa held the wreath, with Tempo perched on her head.

"The wreath was found by these visitors from far away, and their bird of peace," the priest said.

The princes bowed to the Timekeepers.

"Thank you, strangers," said the Prince of Athens. He turned to the Spartan prince. "I apologize."

"I accept your apology. Please accept mine," said the Prince of Sparta. "The success and honor of the Games is more important than any argument."

"Peace is restored," said the priest, taking the wreath from Rosa.

The Athenian prince smiled. "Imagine how the Olympic message of peace would spread if people from all lands were able to compete in our Games!"

The Timekeepers tried not to smile. "If they only knew," whispered Rosa.

The priest announced, "We will not wait for the crowning ceremony. This wreath belongs with its rightful owner." He set it on the Prince of Sparta's head.

The Spartan spectators roared their delight, clapping and stamping. Even the Athenian fans clapped.

"Mission accomplished," Rosa said happily. "The Olympic Games are back on track."

"Cuckoo!" Tempo squawked.

"I'm glad we—" Kingsley tailed off. "DeLay!" he cried, pointing to the time thief, who was creeping into the arena.

"Cuckoo!" Tempo took off and flew at DeLay. She circled his head, squawking and shrieking so loudly that everyone looked.

DeLay shook his fist at her and shouted angrily at Rosa and Kingsley. "You— you—"

A man ran to the priest and pointed at DeLay. "Thief! He's the one who stole my chariot!"

"It's true," Kingsley said. "He pushed the driver out."

The priest was furious. "Unless you leave right now," he told DeLay, "your punishment will be to clean all the horse manure out of the stables. Go!"

"You think you've won," DeLay snarled. "But I'll be back!"

A burst of thick black smoke surrounded DeLay. There was a clanging sound, like the chiming of every clock there had ever been. When the smoke cleared, DeLay had gone—back to somewhere in time.

"That's disappointing," Kingsley said. "I wanted to see him shovelling poop!"

The Timekeepers were invited to a feast that night. They sampled everything! There was bread made with barley, and ripe figs served with creamy yogurt, chopped nuts, and honey. Kingsley liked the goat's milk cheese, but Rosa preferred the tangier cheese made from sheep's milk.

"It's a bit different from home, isn't it?" Rosa said. "Speaking of home, we should be going. Where's Tempo?"

Kingsley laughed. "She's had her beak in a bowl of figs for the last ten minutes. Tempo!" he called. "Back to the History Hub, please!"

"Cuckoo!" She wiped her beak on a bread crust and led the Timekeepers away from everyone. She circled their heads, slowly at first, then faster and faster, until she was just a blur. There was a bright white flash Rosa felt a shiver run through her, then the whiteness vanished.

They were back in the History Hub.

The other Timekeepers greeted Rosa and Kingsley, asking questions excitedly.

"Did the wheel stay on?"

"Did you win the race?"

"Did DeLay cause trouble?"

"Hey!" said Jackson. "Look in the display case."

Sarah opened it and took out a postcard. "This is amazing!" she cried.

Everyone crowded around. A drawning had appeared showed Kingsley and Rosa in the middle of the race.

"Look at you go! That's so cool!" said Hannah.

"It was kinda scary," Rosa said.

"More than a bit." Kingsley laughed as he added the postcard to the 'Moments In Time' wall display.

The game! Rosa remembered. "I must go," she said. "Thanks for sharing our Olympics adventure, Kingsley. See you all soon!"

She pressed a button on her watch. White light surrounded her, and Rosa barely had time to take a deep breath before she was back on the soccer field. The last few seconds were ticking away and the ball was coming straight at her. There was no time to control it and line up a shot.

Instead, Rosa kicked the ball with the inside of her left foot, curving it towards the goal.

The keeper went the wrong way.

"GOAL!"

Cheers rang around the stadium. Rosa's teammates hugged her. They'd won the tournament! They were champions, the stars of the season!

When Rosa collected her medal, the mayor congratulated her. "Great goal!" she said. "Keep on like that and one day you'll be in the Olympics!"

Rosa thanked her. *You don't know it, she thought, but I already have been!*

Rosa's
TIMEKEEPER JOURNAL

The ancient Olympics began in the year 776 BCE and ran until 393 CE, when they were banned by a Roman Emperor. Many years later, the modern Olympic games were reborn in Athens, Greece in 1896. Today, we host the games every four years.

The Ancient Olympics

The Ancient Olympic Games took place in Olympia, on the island of Elis, every four years in honor of the king of the Greek gods, Zeus. Around 50,000 people came from all over the Greek world to watch and take part.

Only men were allowed to take part in the Games, and most of the competitiors were soldiers.

The prizes
Today, Olympic champions win gold, silver, and bronze medals, but at the ancient Olympics winners were awarded a wreath of olive tree leaves, and were welcomed back to their homes as heroes.

The Olympic Truce
The ancient Greeks realized that the Olympics had potential for peace, so a sacred truce took place around the games that stated that nobody travelling to the Olympics was allowed to be harmed. These temporary truces were known as "Ekecheiria" which translates to 'the holding of hands'.

The ancient
EVENTS

The ancient Greeks competed in a number of challenging events at the ancient Olympics. Some variations of these events still continue at the modern olympics today!

Chariot race
This was one of the most dangerous but thrilling Olympic events. It took place in a special arena called a Hippodrome, where chariots pulled by horses would race around the track 12 times.

Stadion
The stadion was a foot race, similar to the sprint at the Olympics today. In it, the competitors had to race one length of the stadium, which was around 160 ft (190 m).

The length of the Stadion was said to be the length that the god Heracles could run in a single breath!

Hoplite race

This was another footrace that was introduced in 520 BCE. Athletes had to run two lengths of the stadium while wearing the armorr of the Greek hoplite soldier. It was a test of stamina and speed.

Pentathlon

This five-part contest consisted of a footrace, long jump, discus throw, and javelin throw. Then ended with a wrestling match between the athletes who performed the best in the previous four events.

Athens Vs.
SPARTA

Ancient Greece was made up of different city states. The states had different leaders, but shared the same language, believed in the same gods, and enjoyed many of the same leisure activities. However, there were often big disagreements...

A ferocious feud
One of the fiercest rivalries in Ancient Greece was between Sparta and Athens, the two most powerful city states who were often in conflict or at odds.

Sparta
The Spartans were a nation of legendary warriors. Almost all men served in the nation's army, and men were raised to be soldiers from childhood.

Athens

Athens was the largest
and most influential Greek
state. It was the birthplace
of democracy, and home
to great scientists and
thinkers. The Athenians
also had a powerful navy.

Athens is now the capital
city of modern Greece.

The Peloponnesian War

The Peloponnesian War began in
431 BCE. It was a battle for power
between Athens and Sparta. Sparta
eventually gained victory in 404 BCE.

Quiz

1: What object does DeLay steal?

2: True or false: The sacred truce at the ancient Olympics was called the Ekecheiria.

3: Which two Greek states were arguing during the story?

4: True or false: Episkyros was an ancient version of baseball.

5: Which famous Greek god has a statue featured in the story?

6: Which Greek goddess is known as the goddess of victory?

7: True or false: Horse races took place in something called a Hippodrome.

Glossary

Athens
One of the biggest and most powerful city states in ancient Greece.

Chariot
A horse drawn vehicle used in ancient times.

Ekecheiria
A special truce at the ancient Olympics.

Episkyros
An ancient Greek ball game.

Hippodrome
A stadium used for horse races.

Hoplite
A type of race at the ancient Olympics where the athletes ran in armor.

Incense
A substance burned to produce a pleasant smell.

Lyre
A stringed musical instrument from ancient Greece.

Papyrus
A material similar to paper that was used as a surface to write on.

Podium
The place where athletes are awarded prizes at the Olympics.

Reins
Ropes that a rider holds on to when riding a horse.

Rhapsode
A poet in ancient Greece.

Spectator

People who gather to watch a show, event, or other performance.

Sparta

One of the biggest and most powerful city states in ancient Greece. Known as a nation of powerful warriors.

Stadium

A building where sports and other events take place.

Time Crunch

A magic device used by DeLay to control the flow of time.

Wreath

An arrangement of flowers or leaves. Often used for decoration or to mark an occasion.

Quiz Answers

1. The champion's wreath
2. True
3. Athens and Sparta
4. False
5. Zeus
6. Nike
7. True

For Lily and Rhys

Text for DK by Working Partners Ltd
9 Kingsway, London WC2B 6XF
With special thanks to Lucy Courtenay

Design by Collaborate Ltd
Illustrator Esther Hernando
Consultant Anita Ganeri
Acquisitions Editor James Mitchem
Editors Becca Arlington, Abi Maxwell
US Senior Editor Shannon Beatty
Designers Ann Cannings, Rachael Prokic, Elle Ward
Jacket and Sales Material Coordinator Magda Pszuk
Senior Production Editor Dragana Puvavic
Production Controller Leanne Burke
Publishing Director Sarah Larter

First American Edition, 2023
Published in the United States by DK Publishing
1745 Broadway, 20th Floor, New York, NY 10019
Text copyright © Working Partners Ltd 2023
Layout, illustration, and design copyright © 2023 Dorling
Kindersley Limited.

A Penguin Random House Company
23 24 25 26 27 10 9 8 7 6 5 4 3 2 1
001–327030–Sept/2023

Published in Great Britain by Dorling Kindersley Limited
A catalog record for this bookis available from the Library of Congress.
ISBN: 978-0-7440-6332-5 (Paperback)
ISBN: 978-0-7440-6334-9 (Hardcover)

DK books are available at special discounts when purchased in bulk
for sales promotions, premiums, fund-raising, oreducational use.
For details, contact:
DK Publishing Special Markets,
1745 Broadway, 20th Floor, New York, NY 10019
SpecialSales@dk.com

Printed and bound in Great Britain by
Clays Ltd, Elcograf S.p.A.

For the curious
www.dk.com

THE TIMEKEEPERS

First Flight

Contents

Chapter 1

Flying back in time

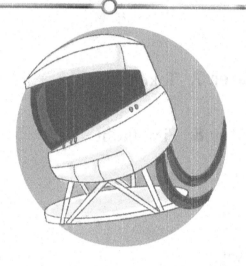

Yasmin battled to hold the joystick straight. The wind was pushing hard, and visibility was bad. Rain lashed across the windshield as she fought to keep the plane under control. There was the runway! She could do this. Putting both hands on the joystick she eased it away

from her. The nose of the plane smoothly
dipped down. The ground was coming
closer… closer… She felt a gentle bump
as the wheels touched down. It was a
perfect landing! Smiling to herself, Yasmin
took off her headset and shook out her
hair. She had always wanted to fly, and
now she had flown.

Well, almost. This was just a flight simulator at an air show near her home in Karachi, Pakistan, and she hadn't really been battling the elements. But it felt like she had, and that's what counted. *One day I'll do it for real,* she thought to herself as she opened the flight simulator door.

"How did that feel?" asked her mom, as Yasmin joined her parents.

"Amazing," said Yasmin honestly. "I could do it all day."

Her dad smiled and took her hand. "There are some wonderful planes here, Yasmin. You're going to love it! We've just got time to see some exhibits before the air display."

There were planes on display from the whole history of human flight. They stood proudly around the hangar, with big signs that told the visitors all about them. There was a British Spitfire from World War II, and one of the earliest jet airplanes. There were biplanes with their two sets of wings, and a great bulky bomber painted with camouflage. Yasmin ran among them, reading about their histories and imagining herself behind the controls, up in the sky.

She stopped at a replica of the first plane to make a powered flight—the Wright Flyer, built by Orville and Wilbur Wright in 1903. Yasmin closed her eyes and imagined how it must have felt to be the first people in the world to make a flight like that! Not gliding, but real, actual *flying*.

She suddenly felt a whirring on her wrist. She glanced down at her special Timekeepers watch. The hands had started to spin—*backward*. Yasmin felt a rush of excitement. She was being called to the History Hub!

Yasmin had a wonderful secret. *She could go back in time.* She was one of the Timekeepers—a secret organization that kept the course of history on track! They had so much fun, traveling into the past and making sure that everything happened the way it was supposed to. But they always had to watch out for a villain named DeLay, who liked messing around with history a little too much...

Yasmin felt worried as well as excited as she gazed at her watch. The Timekeepers were only summoned when DeLay was causing trouble. They were the only ones who could stop him! What was he up to now?

She flipped up the watch face to reveal a hidden screen of buttons. Then she glanced over at her parents, who were reading the information beside an old seaplane. Time wouldn't move while she was away, so her parents wouldn't be worried. But it was good to know that they were enjoying themselves right now.

Yasmin took a deep breath and touched a button on the watch. The hands spun faster. Everything around her stopped, so Yasmin felt as if she was inside a photograph. There was a whirl of rainbow colors as her feet lifted off the ground. Then everything went white.

Yasmin blinked and shook her head. She was standing in a large museum, crammed from floor to ceiling with objects from throughout history, from early flint tools to modern smartphones. This was the History Hub: the Timekeepers' HQ.

"Yasmin, here!" she said. She headed over to her favorite section of the museum to wait for the others. *Coding has come a loooong way,* she thought, as she gazed at the boxy computer screens and heavy keyboards on display.

"Cuckoo! Cuckoo!"
squawked a familiar voice.

Yasmin glanced up at
the large clock on the wall.
It had a swinging pendulum and was
decorated like a gingerbread house.
Just above the clockface, there was a
door—and out of the door peeped
a little bird, sitting on a comfy nest.

Yasmin smiled. "Hi, Tempo!"

Tempo ruffled her striped feathers.
"Cuckoo!" she said again.

Flashes of light began to appear
all around Yasmin as the other
Timekeepers arrived.

"Luke, here!" called a tall boy in a
beautiful handmade poncho. Luke loved
fashion. Yasmin never knew what he

12

would be wearing from one mission to the next!

A girl in paint-spattered overalls appeared. "Hannah, here!" Hannah was the Timekeepers' art expert.

"Jackson, here!" A boy arrived in a cloud of white flour, waving his hand and coughing a little. He was still wearing his baking apron.

"Sarah, here!" Sarah was a girl whose pockets bristled with pens and notebooks. She knew about the authors and poets of the past.

"Rosa, here!" Rosa wiped her hands down her brightly colored soccer uniform. She looked like she had been in the middle of a match!

A boy adjusted the guitar slung over his shoulder and smiled amiably at the others. "Kingsley, here!"

"Min-Jun, here—and sticky!" Min-Jun declared,

14

gingerly holding his latest model between two fingers: a freshly glued plane.

The Timekeepers gathered around the display case in the center of the museum. Whatever appeared inside would give them a clue about their next adventure.

What will it be today? Yasmin wondered. *And which two Timekeepers will the History Hub choose for the mission?*

A little ball of light began to grow inside the display case and an object appeared. It looked like…

"Is that a weather vane?" said Yasmin.

"Maybe?" said Min Jun.

"Whatever it is, it's going to help us beat DeLay," said Luke, and the others all murmured in agreement.

There was a fluttering of wings. Yasmin felt the light brush of Tempo's feathers as the cuckoo settled briefly on her shoulder.

"Yes!" she cried. "I'm on this mission. Who's with me?"

Tempo fluttered up and swooped around a couple of times before landing a little clumsily on Min-Jun's head.

"Me, by the look of things," said Min-Jun, laughing as he peered up through his fringe.

"Cuckoo!" said Tempo.

The little bird jumped off Min-Jun
and flew toward the display case,
where she settled and started preening
her feathers.

Yasmin opened the display-case door
and carefully took out the strange object.
It did look like a weather vane, with a
long stem topped with four cups, tilted
sideways to catch the wind. But Yasmin
knew from experience that things weren't
always as they seemed. She put the object
in her backpack.

Tempo flew on to Yasmin's shoulder. She always accompanied the Timekeepers on their missions. "Cuckoo!" she squawked with excitement.

"Good to have you with us, Tempo," said Min-Jun with a grin.

"We can always use a helping wing!" Yasmin joked.

"Cuckoo!" said Tempo cheerfully.

The other Timekeepers opened their watches to reveal six screens, ready to help Yasmin and Min-Jun if they needed it. Tempo began to fly around Yasmin and Min-Jun, faster and faster, until the stripes on her feathers blurred into wide, sweeping circles. Light burst around them.

FLASH!

Yasmin blinked away the last dancing
spots of light. The first thing she noticed
was the fresh, clean smell of the ocean,
and the roar of waves crashing against a
sandy shore. She looked down at her long
brown skirt and neatly pinned blue
blouse. She had a hat on her head, and
stout leather boots on her feet.

Min-Jun was wearing pants, a light-colored shirt and a waistcoat. He pushed the checked woolen cap back off his head and grinned at Yasmin. "Great outfit," he said. "When are we?"

"Cuckoo!" said Tempo, still perched on Yasmin's shoulder.

Yasmin checked her watch. "It's 1903, and we're in Kitty Hawk, in North Carolina," she said slowly. "Hey! That's where the Wright brothers flew their first—"

"Watch out!" Min-Jun suddenly shouted.

Yasmin looked up from her watch. A plane was skidding across the sand, heading right toward them!

Chapter 2

"Tarnation!"

Clouds of sand whirled in the air as the plane thundered toward them. Yasmin and Min-Jun were deafened by the roar of an enormous propeller. They threw themselves out of the way just in time. It was hard in these old-fashioned clothes, and Yasmin's skirt tangled around her legs

as she scrambled up a nearby sand dune.
Min-Jun was close behind her. He had
lost his hat.

"Cuckoo!" shouted Tempo in alarm.
"Cuckoo! Cuckoo!"

With a final sputtering sound from the propeller, everything fell quiet. The dust and sand settled. Yasmin and Min-Jun sank on to the dune and stared at the amazing machine in front of them.

It looked nothing like a modern plane. It had a wooden framework that reminded Yasmin of Min-Jun's model, and two sets of wide canvas wings, one on top of the other, separated by rows of wooden struts. There were two large wooden propellers, and what looked like a small engine fixed above the pilot. The pilot wasn't seated, like Yasmin had expected, but lying down on his front.

"Tarnation!" the pilot cried in disappointment. Clearly the flight hadn't gone to plan.

"I was *going* to say," Yasmin told Min-Jun as she caught her breath, "that Kitty Hawk is where the Wright brothers made the first-ever powered flight, in 1903."

"Awesome!" said Min-Jun, looking at the plane on the sand in front of them with admiration.

"Cuckoo," said Tempo, looking a bit ruffled.

"Wilbur! Hey, Wilbur!" Another man came running toward the plane, his scarf flying behind him. "Did you damage the plane?"

"You're more worried about the
Flyer than about me, Orville," said the
pilot a little grumpily. "I'm doing just
fine, thanks for asking."

Yasmin wanted to shout with
excitement. It was the Wright
brothers themselves!

It looked like Wilbur was struggling to take off his harness. Yasmin and Min-Jun ran down the dune to offer help.

"I'm sorry for almost hitting you there," apologized the pilot as he finally wriggled out of his seat and dropped down on to the sand. "You appeared out of nowhere! How do you do? I'm Wilbur Wright, and that's my brother, Orville."

Orville Wright had reached the plane. He breathlessly tipped his bowler hat at Yasmin and Min-Jun. "Thanks for your help, uh…?"

Yasmin and Min-Jun introduced themselves. Min-Jun had found his hat at the bottom of the dune, and tipped it politely the way Orville Wright had done.

"We're just, ah, visiting this beach today," Min-Jun said. That much was true, at least!

"Well, we hope you don't think too badly of the place," said Wilbur as he dusted sand off his waistcoat.

"What's wrong with your—"Yasmin began. Just in time she remembered that nobody in 1903 would know what the Flyer was. Even the word 'plane' would be wrong. "…machine?" she finished.

"Darned if I know," confessed Wilbur.

Orville scratched his head as he and his brother looked the Flyer over.

"Rudder's in the wrong position, I reckon," said Orville finally.

Wilbur's expression cleared. "No wonder it wouldn't take off. One of the propellers stopped working mid-flight, too.

Just the strangest thing. One minute it
was turning, the next minute—nothing."

They all jumped as a whirring sound
started up from the grounded plane. A
propeller had started turning, as if it had
heard Wilbur talking about it. The Wright
brothers stared.

"Will you look at that!" said Orville
in surprise.

Yasmin and Min-Jun shared a look. Things stopping and starting again for no reason? That sounded like a Time Crunch—a moment when time froze, or repeated, or fast-forwarded. There was only one person who used Time Crunches to cause this kind of mischief. DeLay! The arch time villain was somewhere nearby...

"We need to get the Flyer back to the hangar," Orville was saying to his brother.

"Need some help?" offered Min-Jun.

Yasmin and Min-Jun helped Orville and Wilbur tow the Flyer back up the beach. It was pretty light for an aircraft, but it was still hard work. Yasmin and Min-Jun had to stop a few times to wipe their foreheads. Tempo flew overhead, calling, "Cuckoo! Cuckoo!" in encouragement.

"Nice bird," said Orville, shading his eyes as he looked up at Tempo swooping and circling.

"Studying how birds fly has really helped us build our flying machines," said Wilbur. "See how your bird uses her wings?"

Yasmin gazed at the way Tempo tilted her wings to catch the ocean breeze. There were no trees for miles in Kitty Hawk, and the steady north to north-east winds consistently sweeping the beach made it a great place for the Wright brothers' flying attempts. She nodded.

"Same thing with the Flyer," said Wilbur proudly, patting the machine. "Our first experiments were with gliders up in the old lighthouse. Then we added an engine, to see if we could get moving with something more than just the power of the wind. We're making progress."

"We think the Flyer might be the one," Orville added. "Once we sort out the rudder."

They reached the Wrights' hangar
and helped carry the Flyer inside. Yasmin
gazed around at the wide open space,
with the smaller workshop to one side.
There were clamps and saws, wrenches,
and scattered pieces of timber; rolls of
canvas fabric, and engine parts scattered
on tabletops. There was even a glider,
lying quietly on its side with one fabric-
covered wing tilted toward the roof.

"Pass me a wrench, Wilbur," said Orville, holding out a hand. "I need to take a closer look at that rudder."

Yasmin and Min-Jun sat on a bench that stood against the wall of the hangar and watched the Wright brothers at work. Tempo found a comfortable perch in the rafters and happily shouted, "Cuckoo!" every few minutes.

"Hey," said Orville suddenly, wriggling out from beneath the Flyer. "What time's the supply boat due in?"

Wilbur glanced at a large clock on the rough wooden wall. "Any minute," he said. "Reckon we'll be late if we don't go right away."

Yasmin exchanged a glance with Min-Jun. This was a great opportunity to start looking for DeLay! She jumped up. "Can we help?"

"Could you go meet the boat?" said
Wilbur. He wiped his face with the back
of his hand, leaving a smear of oil on his
forehead. "If we don't pick up our
supplies, we'll be pretty stuck. It would be
very kind of you."

Yasmin was surprised. She thought
Kitty Hawk had a bridge to the
mainland. Why did the Wrights need a
boat? Then she realized the bridge hadn't
been built in 1903.

"Where does the boat come in?"
Min-Jun asked.

"A couple of miles down the beach,"
said Orville. "Take our bicycles, if you
want. Do you ride?"

Yasmin and Min-Jun both nodded.

"We made them ourselves," said
Wilbur with pride, showing them two
bicycles propped up outside the hangar.
"We had a bike shop, back in Ohio. Our
sister Katherine still runs that."

"We designed the Flyer with these in mind, as well as birds," said Orville. He patted Yasmin's handlebars. "The Flyer leans and banks, just the same as our bicycles."

"Cool," said Min-Jun.

Wilbur frowned. "Yes, I suppose the wind is a little chilly."

"But once you start cycling, you'll soon warm up!" added Orville.

Yasmin stifled a giggle. The Wrights thought Min-Jun was talking about the weather!

She and Min-Jun cycled away down the beach to get the supplies with Tempo flying overhead. DeLay was around here somewhere. It was time to track him down…

Time Crunch

The bicycles were heavier and bumpier
than Yasmin and Min-Jun were used to.
They didn't have modern bicycle
suspensions to cushion them as they
rattled along. There were no gears either,
so it was hard work. But the machinery
was well-oiled and the pedals turned

easily. They cycled down a wooden
boardwalk, passing beaches and dunes.

"Cuckoo!" Tempo swooped happily
over their heads, enjoying the ocean wind
beneath her wings.

A lighthouse stood in the distance,
black and white, looking out to sea. To
Yasmin's delight, there were herds of wild
horses grazing among the dune grasses
and galloping along the sand. And all the
while, a breeze was blowing in from the
Atlantic Ocean, keeping them cool.

She was having so much
fun that she almost forgot to
keep an eye out for DeLay.
Watching Tempo glide and soar reminded
her of their mission—if they didn't stop
the villain, the Wright Brothers wouldn't
make their first flight...

By the time they reached the supply
boat, which had docked at a wide
wooden jetty, they still hadn't spotted any
sign of DeLay.

"We're here for the Wright Brothers'
supplies?" said Min-Jun breathlessly.

Two boxes were loaded on to the
back of the bicycles. Yasmin suppressed a
small groan at the thought of cycling
back again. The bicycles were even
heavier now!

"Cuckoo!" Tempo chirped in encouragement as they set off.

"Easy for you to say!" said Min-Jun, huffing and puffing.

By the time they arrived back at the hangar, their cheeks glowed. "Good old Katherine!" exclaimed Wilbur as the brothers eagerly unpacked the boxes. There was flour, and apples, a can of oil, several cans of beans, a package of letters, and even a bag of orange and yellow candies. "I don't know where we'd be without her!"

"Want some candy?" Orville offered, holding out the sweets.

"We couldn't manage without our sister," said Wilbur. "We already told you she keeps our bicycle shop running back in Ohio, right?"

"And more besides," said Orville. "She's wonderful at telling people about our work, and keeping us organized."

"I've heard of Katherine Wright," Yasmin whispered to Min-Jun as they leaned against the wall of the hangar, munching on the candy. "She traveled all over the world with her brothers, representing the Wright company."

"Does your bird like apples?" said Wilbur. He cut a slice off an apple and offered it to Tempo.

Tempo fluttered down from her perch in the rafters and took the apple slice. But then…

"Cuckoo!" she cried, spitting out the treat. "Cuckoo, cuckoo!"

"What…?" said Wilbur.

They all gazed at the apple slice lying on the floor. The edges were curling up as they watched. The once-crisp apple flesh shriveled and developed spots of blue mold. It was rotting away, right before their eyes.

Yasmin swung around and stared at the rest of the supplies.

The bag of flour had collapsed, with a bloom of green mold developing around the bottom. The cans of beans were rusting, bending… breaking open right in front of her. She caught Min-Jun's eye. This was bad. DeLay was here, messing around with his Time Crunches again and changing how time works. He might even be inside the hangar itself, causing mischief with the planes!

The Wrights were still staring at the rotten apple.

"Can you please show us your flying machines?" Min-Jun blurted, before Orville and Wilbur could turn around and

48

see the mess that DeLay had made with the rest of the supplies.

The frown on Orville's face cleared. He smiled at Min-Jun and Yasmin. "Sure! Follow me."

They left the workshop and entered the yawning space of the hangar. Everything was quiet. Dust danced in the air, and there were little heaps of sand in the corners, blown in from Kitty Hawk beach.

"Wilbur fixed the rudder," Orville said proudly as they approached the Flyer, which stood by itself near the entrance to the hangar. "I reckon we'll get the Flyer in the air the next time the wind is right."

Yasmin and Min-Jun looked at the Flyer. There was a feeling of unease in Yasmin's belly. Something was different, she thought with a frown. She couldn't put her finger on it, but it looked – slightly lopsided.

Wilbur gave a sharp cry of dismay. "Where's the second propeller?" he said.

Yasmin's eyes widened. No wonder the Flyer looked lopsided. Instead of two propellers—one on each side of the pilot's seat—there was only one!

DeLay was up to his old tricks. He
was trying to stop the first powered flight
from ever taking place.

Chapter 4

Down with DeLay!

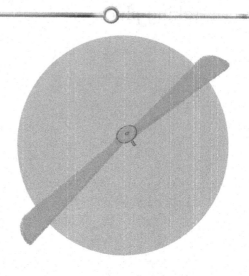

The Wright brothers hunted all over the hangar for the propeller. No luck. Yasmin and Min-Jun felt awful.

"We need that propeller," said Orville.

"Without it, we'll never get the Flyer off the ground!" said Wilbur.

Yasmin and Min-Jun looked at each

other. There was often a moment in the Timekeepers' missions when they had to explain about DeLay without mentioning time travel. Telling people about that could change history, and that was NOT what the Timekeepers were here to do.

"This is going to sound kind of strange," Min-Jun began.

"Stranger than a propeller disappearing into thin air?" said Wilbur.

Taking turns, Min-Jun and Yasmin

explained about DeLay.

"He's a troublemaker," said Yasmin.

"He messes around with people's lives," said Min-Jun.

"And we think he's trying to stop you from flying!" Yasmin finished. "He's the one who's stolen your propeller. We're sure of it!"

Orville and Wilbur both looked shocked. Orville sank on to a nearby bench with his head in his hands. "This is terrible," he muttered. "Just terrible."

"Maybe it's not so bad," said Min-Jun hopefully. "Can't you just make another one?"

"I wish it was that simple," said Wilbur. "Each propeller is hand-carved. We put so much work into matching the propellers so that the power was evenly distributed. We've carved, and polished, and carved, and polished, and measured, and carved some more. Making sure that our two propellers matched was the hardest thing we've ever done."

"We aren't even sure we have the science right," said Orville sadly. "We're still testing. But we really hoped we'd nailed it this time. We'll never be able to replicate that propeller again."

"And after the failure earlier today, this is the last straw," said Wilbur. He sank down on the bench beside his brother. "Our dream of flying is over. We might as well go back to Ohio and help Katherine sell our bicycles."

Yasmin wanted to yell with frustration. DeLay had stopped the Wrights from conducting the most important experiment in the history of powered flight! Without the success of the Flyer, the world of aviation would never develop. There would be no air show in

Karachi. No flight simulator for Yasmin to explore her own dreams of flying. It was a disaster.

They had to stop DeLay and find that propeller!

"You search the rest of the hangar," Yasmin suggested to Orville and Wilbur. "We'll take a look on the beach."

Yasmin and Min-Jun took the bicycles and pedaled back out into the bright December sunshine. The smell of the sea was rich and salty, and seagulls flew in white circles high in the sky. Tempo swooped around their heads in a worried kind of way.

Yasmin and Min-Jun bumped along the salt-spotted boardwalk, scanning the beach. But apart from the occasional lump of driftwood, there was nothing.

"Cuckoo!" said Tempo suddenly. She flapped her wings extra hard, and soared high into the air. "Cuckoo!"

Yasmin stopped pedaling, resting her feet on the boardwalk. Min-Jun did the same.

"What did you see just now, Tempo?" Yasmin asked.

She and Min-Jun stared down the beach. A group of wild horses were gathered by the water's edge. They stood in a tight circle with their heads down, looking curiously at something.

"Come on," said Yasmin, propping up her bicycle against a piece of fencing. "Let's take a look."

They raced together down the soft sand. One of the horses noticed them, tossed its gray head, and whinnied at the others. The horses were all beautiful, with dappled coats and long, salt-tangled manes. As one, they whirled around and galloped away—revealing…

"It's just another piece of driftwood," said Min-Jun in disappointment.

"It looks more like a tree," Yasmin said.

But as they got closer, Yasmin realized that it wasn't a tree at all.

Min-Jun punched the air. "We beat you already, DeLay!" he said excitedly.

Yasmin couldn't believe DeLay had made it so easy. They were hardly any distance from the hangar—and yet there was no denying it. They were definitely looking at a propeller.

It was easy to see how they had mistaken it for a tree. Someone had stuck it into the ground and tied some branches to the top to disguise it. Yasmin inspected it curiously. She had no idea propellers were so big. This one towered over them, standing a good eight feet high.

Yasmin gave it a tug. It tilted slightly. "Come on Min-Jun, help me!" she said.

They pulled off the fake branches and tugged at the enormous object until it fell flat on to the sand. Just like Wilbur had said, it was carved from a single piece of wood, with a twisting shape designed to catch the wind as it turned. Yasmin took one end and Min-Jun took the other. They had beaten DeLay already! The Wrights would make their famous flight after all—maybe even that very afternoon.

"Down with DeLay," sang Yasmin as she and Min-Jun carried the propeller blade up the beach. "Hey, hey, hey! Down with DeLay!"

"Koo-Koo-cuckoo-koo!" shouted Tempo joyfully from her perch on top of Yasmin's head.

"This must be the fastest Timekeepers mission ever," Min-Jun joked. They balanced the propeller carefully across their bikes, and started pushing it back up the boardwalk.

"You'd think DeLay would come up with a better plan than this!" agreed Yasmin with a grin. "I can't wait to see Wilbur and Orville's faces."

The brothers were waiting anxiously in their workshop. Yasmin and Min-Jun wheeled the propeller proudly into the hangar.

"Ta da!" said Yasmin with a flourish. "One propeller."

"Oh," said Orville.

"Oh no," said Wilbur.

Yasmin exchanged a look of surprise with Min-Jun. This wasn't the reaction they were expecting.

"Is there a problem?" said Min-Jun.

If anything, the brothers looked more defeated than before.

"It's an old propeller," said Wilbur.

"That didn't work," said Orville.

All the feelings of pride and triumph oozed out of Yasmin. She should have known. Finding it had been way too easy. DeLay must have stolen the old propeller to trick them. They had fallen right into his time-meddling hands.

"Cuckoo," said Tempo sadly. Her feathers looked like they were drooping.

"We hunted all over the hangar, the workshop and the yards outside," said Orville. "There is no sign of it anywhere."

"Thanks for your help," said Wilbur quietly. "But I think it's time my brother and I went back home to Ohio. There's nothing here for us any more."

Chapter 5

A helping wing

"We can't let Orville and Wilbur give up,"
said Yasmin in determination as they
cycled back down the boardwalk. "It's
too important."

"Cuckoo," agreed Tempo, perched on
Yasmin's handlebars. The ocean breeze
was blowing her feathers around, so she

looked more like a mop
than a bird.

"They seem pretty
certain that they couldn't do it
without that propeller," said
Min-Jun gloomily.

"I think it's time to call the others,"
said Yasmin. "They may have
some ideas."

They wheeled their bicycles in among
the sand dunes, to get out of the wind.
Then they laid them down carefully on
the sandy ground, and pushed up their
sleeves. Their special Timekeeper
watches blinked at them. Yasmin and
Min-Jun both flipped them up, and
pressed a button.

The other Timekeepers appeared: a tiny gallery of faces on the screens concealed inside the watches.

"Hey there," said Kingsley.

"How's it going?" asked Rosa. She still had a speck of mud on her nose.

"Not great," Yasmin confessed. "DeLay has stolen a propeller from the Wright brothers' plane. We can't find it anywhere. They're talking about giving up and going home to Ohio before they've made the first powered flight in history."

Sarah looked concerned. "You've looked everywhere you can think of?"

"There's too much ground to cover," said Min-Jun. "Kitty Hawk beach is enormous. The propeller could be anywhere. And we've only got a couple of bicycles between us."

"I wish we could borrow a plane to cover a wider area," said Yasmin gloomily. "But we can't borrow a plane which hasn't been invented yet!"

The other Timekeepers looked thoughtful.

Tempo started pecking Yasmin's watch screen. "Cuckoo," she said. She sounded insistent. "Cuckoo, cuckoo!"

"Tempo!" said Sarah suddenly. "That's it!"

"What do you mean?" asked Min-Jun.

Tempo spread her wings and flapped them vigorously, clinging to Yasmin's arm.

"Humans may not be able to fly yet," Sarah said, "but Tempo can!"

"Cuckoo!" shouted Tempo. *Finally*, she seemed to be saying!

"Of course!" exclaimed Min-Jun.

Yasmin rolled her eyes at herself. They'd had a perfect flying machine all along, and hadn't even realized it!

"Thanks guys," she said gratefully. "You're the best."

The others waved and disappeared. The screens on Yasmin and Min-Jun's watches went dark.

"Looks like this is up to you, Tempo,"

Yasmin said to the little cuckoo perched
on her arm. "Fly up as high as you can,
and tell us if you see anything!"

"Up," said Min-Jun, pointing helpfully
at the mass of clouds in the December
sky. "Up!"

Tempo cocked her head. Then she
spread her wings and took off, spiraling
up into the sky until she was just a striped
dot far above their heads. Down on the

sand dunes, Yasmin and Min-Jun exchanged a high-five, hopped back on to their bicycles and followed her.

Now they just had to hope that the little cuckoo would find the clue they all needed so desperately.

It was difficult to keep track of Tempo as she flew. But every now and then, she swooped down, to check that they were still following. The waves crashed on the shore, sweeping up and down the sand as Yasmin and Min-Jun pedaled along.

Yasmin concentrated on keeping the wheels of her bicycle away from the sand. They were nearing the lighthouse again. She remembered seeing it on their ride to the supply boat.

Tempo fluttered down in a whoosh
of striped feathers.

"Anything yet, Tempo?"
asked Min-Jun.

"Cuckoo!" said Tempo.

She rocketed right up into the sky
again. Yasmin stopped the bike and
shaded her eyes to keep track.

"She's heading for the lighthouse,"
said Min-Jun suddenly.

Sure enough, Yasmin saw Tempo land
on the top of the lighthouse.

The little bird stretched out her wings and flapped them urgently. "Cuckoo!" she cried. "Cuckoo!"

"Do you think there's something up there?" Yasmin asked Min-Jun.

Min-Jun had stopped his bike too. He pushed back his hat and squinted at the lighthouse. "She's being pretty loud," he observed.

"CUCKOO!" shouted Tempo. She circled the lighthouse once, twice, three times, and landed again at the very top. "CUCKOO!"

Excitement stirred in Yasmin's belly. "She's definitely seen something," she said, getting back on to her bike.

A path led down from the

74

boardwalk to the lighthouse. It was
narrower than the main route, and a lot
bumpier, so Yasmin and Min-Jun pedaled
carefully. Propping their bicycles against
the weathered wooden lighthouse door,
they tried the handle. The door
creaked open.

The space inside was small and dusty,
with a rickety spiral staircase that curled
up toward the light at the very top. They
could still hear Tempo cuckooing
loudly outside.

The staircase was tight and twisted. Yasmin took the lead, with Min-Jun following up the creaky wooden treads. Yasmin felt quite dizzy by the time they reached the top.

The top of the lighthouse was flooded with light. Yasmin stared at the waves crashing far below, and the wide blue horizon of the Atlantic Ocean. She wondered what it would be like to be up here on a stormy night.

"Look!" Min-Jun shouted.

Yasmin tore her eyes from the view. Lying in the middle of the circular space at the top of the lighthouse was something long and wooden, with a familiar carved and twisted shape. The propeller!

"So you've found it at last," said a horribly familiar voice.

Yasmin and Min-Jun whirled around. A tall, bony figure stood at the top of the lighthouse stairs. He wore a long robe decorated with hourglasses, which flapped around him as if caught in a strong wind. His hair writhed on his head like a nest of wild white snakes. His eyes gleamed like flat, wet pebbles.

Yasmin gasped. It was none other than DeLay himself!

Chapter 6

An escape plan

Time seemed to stand still. Yasmin and
Min-Jun stood frozen and even the waves
outside the lighthouse seemed to fall
silent. Perhaps time really *had* stopped,
Yasmin thought. Stopping time was one
of DeLay's specialties, after all.

The wild-haired villain smiled

mockingly at Yasmin and Min-Jun, and swept a low bow.

"I congratulate you on your persistence," he said. "But you are too late. Even now, those useless brothers are packing up their toys and preparing to head back to Ohio."

"This isn't over yet, DeLay," said Min-Jun fiercely. "We're taking this propeller back, and you can't stop us!"

Tempo zoomed around DeLay's head, squawking furiously.

"Get your little bird under control," said DeLay, scowling. "No one likes a bad loser. There's nothing you can do to stop me this time. TIME! Ha!"

He scooped up the propeller. Then he whirled around and ran for the stairs, his robe billowing behind him in a greasy brown cloud. His hand flicked into his pocket. Yasmin glimpsed him throwing what looked like a small pocket watch and heard a familiar sound. *Tick, tick, tick.* There was a burst of smoke. The top of the lighthouse distorted like a fun house mirror.

"Look out!" Yasmin shouted. "He's thrown a Time Crunch!"

The wood of the top stair began to warp and curl. Just like the apple in the Wrights' workshop, it was aging and rotting before their eyes.

"Follow him!" Min-Jun shouted. He darted for the stairs.

"Cuckoo!" shouted Tempo in warning.

"It's too late, Min-Jun," Yasmin cried. "The stairs aren't safe!"

Min-Jun almost stumbled on the top step as it crumbled to dust. Yasmin pulled him back. The long, twisting spiral below them flaked and groaned, breaking into pieces—until with a resounding **CRACK** it fell away. There was nothing left but a high, yawning space. The Time Crunch had done its deadly work.

DeLay's mocking laughter floated up to them from the ground. "How are you going to get out of this one, hmm? There will be no powered flight today, tomorrow, or EVER. I'm going to enjoy watching those brothers go home as failures! Ha ha ha!"

Yasmin and Min-Jun rushed to the

edge of the platform on the lighthouse roof. DeLay was bounding away, his robe flying out behind him like a witch's cloak. His laughter rolled through their heads like the sound of the crashing waves on the shore.

Min-Jun beat his fist on the rail that encircled the platform they stood on. "I can't believe he got away!" he said, resting his head on his hands. "What are we going to do?"

Yasmin frowned at the skipping, flapping figure of the time villain as he raced away down the beach. "He doesn't

have the propeller anymore," she said. "It must be downstairs."

"Cuckoo!" agreed Tempo.

Min-Jun lifted his head. "So what? We can't get down to retrieve it, wherever he's put it."

Yasmin moved to the other side of the lighthouse. Way off in the distance, she could see the Wright brothers' hangar, and the bustle of activity around its wide, high doors. Orville and Wilbur were packing up their equipment, just as DeLay had predicted.

Yasmin couldn't imagine a world without airplanes. They had to figure out a way to fix this.

"Hey," she said suddenly. "Didn't Wilbur say something about using the lighthouse for some of their early flying experiments?"

"Yes…" Min-Jun said slowly.

Yasmin looked around. There was a lot of stuff on the ground. Most of it was covered in dust sheets or propped up against the curved railings. Maybe there was something here that could help them.

She reached for the nearest dust sheet and tugged. It slithered to the floor, revealing a large roll of canvas. It was very like the material they had seen back in the workshop. In fact, it looked identical.

Yasmin moved to the next dust sheet. This one hid a box of thick sailors' needles and strong-looking thread. The next sheet revealed bundles of wooden struts. "Look at all this!" she said. "It might be just what we need. What's under that big dust sheet over there?"

Min-Jun dashed to the bulky, covered object. Yasmin joined him. Together, they pulled the sheet away. A battered glider

lay before them, made of wood and
canvas. It was dusty, and there were a few
holes in the canvas. One of the wings
looked a little crooked, too. But it was big
enough to carry an adult—or two kids.

"Are you thinking what I'm
thinking?" Yasmin asked with excitement.

"Yes," said Min-Jun, "I think I am."

"We can use this to glide out of here!"
said Yasmin.

Min-Jun sighed. "I think we're
officially crazy."

"It just needs a bit of fixing up," said

Yasmin. "You're the modeling expert. Time to get modeling!"

She grabbed the box with the sailors' needles and thread and passed it to Min-Jun. He threaded a needle and started sewing up the holes in the glider's canvas wings.

Next, Yasmin took off her backpack and put it on the floor. After digging around inside, she pulled out the strange weather vane object they had taken from the History Hub. She still hadn't figured the object out, but she knew it would be useful on their mission. The objects from the History Hub always were.

She stood it upright on the floor.

A strong gust of wind swirled the dust around her feet. Yasmin heard a clicking sound. The weather vane object was clicking gently, spinning where it stood.

Yasmin suddenly realized what it was.

"Anemometer!" she said.

"Bless you," said Min-Jun, threading one of the long sailors' needles with new thread.

Yasmin laughed. "The object we got from the History Hub—it's an anemometer. It measures wind!"

Min-Jun looked up "So how does that help us?"

Yasmin studied the little object. The four sideways cups were spinning briskly now. "It tells us wind speed and direction," she said. "We can use it to judge the direction for launching the glider. There's no point taking off into a head wind. We'll just get blown back. We need a tail wind to push us along. And we need to know the wind speed so we can judge how to use the controls."

Min-Jun bit off his thread and tied a knot. He got to his feet and studied the glider wings. "This thing doesn't really have controls," he said. "Just a pulley system. Do you really think it'll fly?"

"Oh, it'll fly," said Yasmin with confidence. "This is the Wright brothers we're talking about. They figured out the glider before they moved on to their powered flight ideas. Give me a piece of thread, will you?"

Min-Jun passed Yasmin a piece of the sturdy green yarn he had been using to repair the glider wings. Yasmin tied it to the stem of one of the cups. Using her Timekeepers watch, she measured the length of one of the rods that held the cups to the center of the anemometer. "If I double this," she murmured, "I can calculate the diameter of the cups—that's the width—then multiply by pi, or roughly three, to find out the circumference—that's all the way around the circle…"

"You've totally lost me," said Min-Jun.

"I often have that effect," said Yasmin with a grin. She pressed the stopwatch feature on her watch, and timed the cups as they rotated for exactly one minute. "Right," she said, clicking the stopwatch. Using the math she had learned from coding, she ran some swift calculations. "The wind is moving at approximately twenty miles an hour, and coming from the east. If we launch the glider here"— she patted the railing beside her—"then we have the best chance of catching that wind and gliding down to the beach."

"And you can tell all that from those little cups?" said Min-Jun in astonishment.

Yasmin tapped her nose. "Four little cups—and some math, too," she said.

"Cuckoo!" said Tempo, a
bit anxiously.

The theory was good. But would it
work in practice? There was only one
way to find out!

Chapter 7

Takeoff!

Yasmin and Min-Jun took up their
positions, standing up between the glider's
wings. Min-Jun held on with both hands.
Yasmin held on with just one. Her other
hand clutched the anemometer.

"Wait until there's a decent gust of
wind," she warned.

"I'm going nowhere until you say so,"
said Min-Jun. He looked a little pale. The
ground was a long way off.

There was a sudden gust. The
anemometer cups spun vigorously.

"NOW!" shouted Yasmin.

They ran forward, holding on tightly.
As they reached the railings around the
top of the lighthouse, they both jumped,
tucked their legs underneath them and
landed flat on their tummies on
the glider.

There was a lurch as the glider
dropped over the edge. For one horrible
moment, they plunged downward—until,
with a bounce, the wind caught the
underside of the glider's wings and they
leveled out. They'd done it! They
were flying!

"Whoo!" shouted Yasmin.

"Yeah!" roared Min-Jun.

The wind tore at their hair and lashed at their clothes. Yasmin felt like she was catching a ride on an enormous bird.

"Cuckoo!" shouted Tempo happily, flapping her wings beside Yasmin's head as she did her best to keep up with the glider. "Cuckoo!"

Yasmin had judged the wind direction just right. The nose of the glider began to dip, lower and lower, until the wooden runners beneath met the soft sand of the beach. They skidded down the beach, drifting from side to side, until at last—they stopped.

Yasmin threw her arms in the air, giddy with the thrill of the flight. "That was AMAZING!" she shouted.

Min-Jun grinned weakly as he slid off the glider. "Amazing is one way of putting it," he said.

They had landed a short distance from the lighthouse. Yasmin ran back toward the warped wooden door, and the curved wall where their bicycles still stood. She raced inside, hoping DeLay hadn't broken the propeller out of spite.

No! It was still there!

Yasmin took one end. Min-Jun took the other. They carefully carried the propeller outside, and balanced it on the handlebars of the two bicycles, just as they had earlier. Then they wheeled the bicycles back up to the boardwalk and pushed them toward the hangar.

"We need to go faster," Yasmin urged Min-Jun. "I don't want DeLay showing up again and throwing another Time Crunch."

"I'm going as fast as I can!" Min-Jun exclaimed.

It took them fifteen minutes of fast walking and pushing before they reached the hangar. Wilbur and Orville both came running out to meet them.

"You found it!" Orville gasped.

Wilbur did a little happy dance in front of the hangar. "I can't believe it!" he said. "We thought everything was lost and that DeLay guy had won!"

"We had almost packed up the whole workshop," Orville admitted.

Yasmin patted the propeller. "You can still make your flight happen," she said.

Orville grinned broadly. "You're right," he said. "We didn't come this far to give up now."

"You've really inspired us!" said

Wilbur. "If this flight goes as planned,
well…who knows how far humans will
be able to fly one day?"

"Maybe as far as the next town!"
said Orville.

Yasmin and Min-Jun shared a
knowing grin. "Maybe," said
Yasmin, laughing.

Word spread through the small settlement of Kitty Hawk that the Wright brothers were making another attempt to fly their machine down the beach. As the sound of hammering filled the hangar, with Orville and Wilbur reattaching the propeller and Yasmin and Min-Jun helping with a few last-minute adjustments to the Flyer, people started drifting into view. Some came in groups. One or two came alone. Straw hats flapped in the strong winter breeze. Scarves flew like woolen flags around people's necks, and skirts whipped and snapped around the women's legs. There was a sense of anticipation in the air. Tempo sat high up on the top of the hangar, squawking happily.

"I think we're ready," said Wilbur, straightening up from where he had been tightening one of the wires that crisscrossed between the slim wooden struts and held the wings in place. "Just need to check the wind speed. Hey, Orville! Where's the anemometer?"

"I don't know," said Orville, scratching his head. "Maybe we packed it away?"

The brothers looked dismayed.

They needed to know the wind speed and direction or the flight couldn't take place. They couldn't fail now!

"Use ours," Yasmin offered. And she pulled the History Hub anemometer from her bag.

Wilbur looked incredulous. "Where would we be without you two?" he said, shaking his head.

The wind speed had picked up, and was now twenty-seven miles per hour.

"It's a little fast," Wilbur admitted. "But we'll give it our best shot. Hey Orville, want to flip a coin for who gets to be the pilot?"

The brothers tossed a small silver coin. Orville won. Ramming his leather helmet on his head, Orville grinned and climbed aboard. He settled into position, lying down on his front.

"You two better get into the crowd if you want a decent view," said Wilbur. "I think we're about to make history!"

Chapter 8

First flight

Yasmin felt a flutter of excitement as she and Min-Jun joined the crowds down on the beach. The numbers had swelled as word had spread of this latest attempt to conquer the sky. Was this it? Was this the moment? Someone started playing a barrel organ. Someone else had started

selling ice cream. There was a carnival
atmosphere as the residents of Kitty
Hawk prepared to watch something
astonishing happen.

Yasmin heard the throaty roar of an
engine. The nose of the Flyer appeared.
Then the rest of the machine. The
runners lifted off the ground. The whole
machine drove forward into nothing.
And… liftoff!

"Ooh!" cried the crowd. "Aaah!"

Yasmin watched as the Flyer zoomed over her head. She was dimly aware of a man with a camera on legs beside her, bending down and—**SNAP!**—taking a photograph of the moment so that it would be captured for all time. Five seconds in the air…then ten…

The Flyer gently dipped down and skidded to a halt on the sand some way down the beach. It had been airborne for a full twelve seconds. Orville Wright had just made the first powered flight the world had ever seen.

The crowd erupted. They threw their hats in the air, and waved their scarves like banners. What a moment! Yasmin breathed it in. She turned to Min-Jun.

"Mission accomplished," she said with satisfaction.

He nodded with a wide smile. It was time to go.

The children slipped away quietly from the celebrating crowd, and made their way around the side of the hangar. It wouldn't be good for the people of Kitty Hawk to see them vanish into thin air. It would have been one miracle too many.

DeLay was waiting for them, scowling. His white hair blew around his head as he stabbed the air with a long bony finger.

"You might have put history back on track this time, but this isn't the last you've seen of me," he threatened. "I'll be back. And next time, I'll succeed!"

Min-Jun folded his arms. "We're not scared of you, DeLay," he said.

"Whatever you throw at the Timekeepers, we'll be ready!" Yasmin added.

DeLay gave a sly grin. "That's what YOU think. I have time to get it right one day. Plenty of time...HA!"

There was a flash of fire, a cloud of smoke, and the clattering sound of chiming clocks.

Then he vanished, as if he'd never been there at all.

"Cuckoo!" Tempo fluttered down from her perch on the hangar. She zoomed around Min-Jun and Yasmin, around and around in a blur of brown stripes, until Yasmin felt dizzy. Everything went white…

Yasmin felt her feet touch down on the familiar stone floor of the History Hub. Beside her, Min-Jun dusted himself down and offered Yasmin a high-five.

"Cuckoo!" cried Tempo in celebration.

The other Timekeepers ran over.

"Good job!" cried Rosa, patting them both on the back. Dry mud spattered onto the stone floor. "Oops," she added, staring at her muddy hands.

"We knew you'd succeeded," said Hannah with a grin. "We have evidence. Want to see?"

Yasmin spotted a postcard on the History Hub wall. It showed a girl in a long dress and a straw hat, and a boy in a checkered woolen hat, standing on the edge of a photograph showing the Flyer in midair. Yasmin and Min-Jun had been caught by the photographer at Kitty Hawk! Yasmin's heart soared.

"We couldn't have done it without your help," said Min-Jun.

The history of aviation had been well and truly saved.

It was time for everyone to get back to their everyday lives. The Timekeepers waved goodbye to one another, with more cheering and celebration and back-patting.

Yasmin hugged Min-Jun. "Thanks for the needlework, partner," she joked.

Min-Jun laughed. "Thanks for the math! See you next time!"

Yasmin pressed a button on her watch. There was a rainbow flash of light and a sense of flying that reminded her of the glider, before she felt herself touch down. For a moment, she felt as if she were back in Kitty Hawk—because she had arrived back beside the replica of the Flyer. No time had passed at all. But she grinned when she saw the old photograph on the display panel. There she was, standing beside Min-Jun as the Flyer took off. It was the photograph from the History Hub.

"Come on, Yasmin!" her dad called. "The air display is about to begin!"

Yasmin ran out of the hangar with

her parents. There was a huge **BOOM**—
and a line of jets powered overhead,
angling their sleek wings to catch the
bright Karachi sun. Plumes of colored
smoke trailed behind them in lines and
patterns, crisscrossing the blue sky.

Yasmin smiled privately to herself. To
think, she'd been there when it all began!

Yasmin's
TIMEKEEPER JOURNAL

Wilbur, Orville, and Katharine Wright were siblings from Ohio. While history remembers the two brothers as the pioneers of flight, Katharine was also a key member of the dynamic team.

Wilbur Wright
(1867–1912)

Wilbur was a keen inventor from an early age, but also loved sports. An injury stopped him from attending college as an athlete, so he started a business with Orville.

Did you know?
The brothers tossed a coin to see who would fly first, and Orville won.

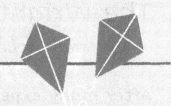

Orville Wright
(1871–1948)

Orville loved flying kites as a child, which may have inspired his love of aviation. He also enjoyed cycling, and along with his siblings, opened a bicycle shop. Their experiments here eventually lead to designs for an aircraft.

Katharine Wright
(1874–1929)

After spending time as a teacher, Katharine Wright ran the Wright's bicycle shop when her brothers focussed on planes. She was also the main contact for her brothers' business dealings, and organized the media events around their flights.

The Wright *FLYER*

After many experiments and attempts, the Wright brothers successfully made the first human-powered flight on December 17, 1903 in an aircraft called the Wright Flyer.

Rudder for steering

Propeller to move the plane forward

40 ft (12 m) wingspan

The first flight only last 12 seconds, but within a few years, a version of the flyer could stay in the air for almost 40 minutes!

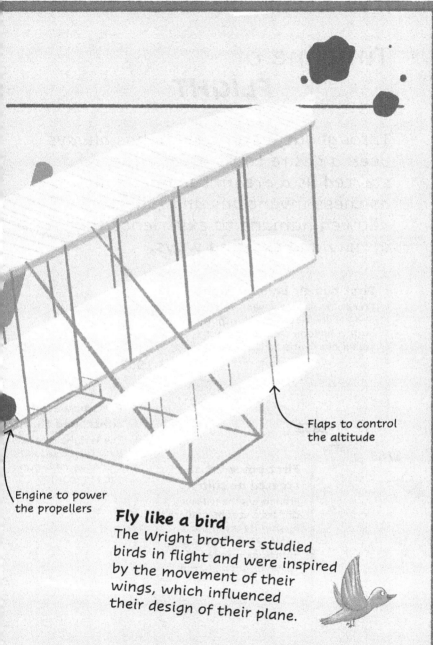

Flaps to control
the altitude

Engine to power
the propellers

Fly like a bird
The Wright brothers studied
birds in flight and were inspired
by the movement of their
wings, which influenced
their design of their plane.

Timeline of
FLIGHT

Throughout history, there has always been a desire to fly. Over time, what started as a dream became reality, as these inventions and milestones allowed humans to experience flight in new and exciting ways.

First hot air balloon flight
French inventors Joseph-Michel and Jacques-Etienne Montgolfier built a balloon from linen, and sailed over Paris for 25 minutes.

1903

First powered, controlled flight
The Wright brothers flew for 12 seconds and covered around 120 ft (30 m).

1852

1783

First powered and steered airship
French engineer Henri Giffard's steam-powered airship flew almost 17 miles (27 km) through France at a speed of around 6 mph (10 kph).

First commercial flight

The world's first regularly scheduled heavier-than-air flight took off from Florida on New Year's Day, 1914.

First flight around the world

A team from the US Army Air Service flew for more than 175 days, landing in 22 different countries along the way.

First human in space

Russian-born Yuri Gagarin became the first person to travel into space, orbiting the Earth for 108 minutes.

1914

1919

1924

1947

1961

First transatlantic flight

British pilots Captain Alcock and Lieutenant Whitten Brown became the first people to fly non-stop across the Atlantic Ocean.

Breaking the speed of sound

U.S. Air Force Captain Chuck Yeager flew faster than the speed of sound, which is 767 mph (1,234 kph).

Quiz

1: What were the names of the two Wright brothers?

2: True or false: the Wright brothers had a sister named Katherine.

3: What device does DeLay use to slow or speed up time?

4: True or false: the Wright brothers made the first human-powered flight in the year 1903.

5: What object does DeLay steal from the Wright brothers?

6: What type of bird is Tempo?

7: True or false: the Wright brothers' plane was called *The Skybird*.

Glossary

Anemometer
A tool used to measure the speed of the wind.

Camouflage
Colors or patterns that help things blend in with their environment.

Canvas
A strong cloth that is often used to make sails or tents.

Dune
Small mounds or ridges of sand formed by the wind or flowing water.

Dust sheet
A piece of cloth used to cover and protect things from dust or paint.

Flight simulator
A machine that recreates the conditions of flight, often used to train pilots.

Gears
A machine part used to increase force or speed.

Glider
A type of aircraft that flies without an engine.

Hangar
A large building where aircraft are stored.

Karachi
A large city in Pakistan.

Pendulum
A weight suspended on a stick or rope, often used in clocks.

Propeller

A mechanical device found in planes or boats that helps create movement.

Plume

A cloud of smoke or dust that looks like a feather.

Rudder

The part of a ship or aircraft that is used to help steer

Spitfire

A British fighter plane used during World War II

Strut

A bar, rod, or brace that helps support a structure.

Time Crunch
A magic device used by DeLay to control the flow of time.

Time travel
The ability to travel back and forward in time to visit the past or future.

Wrench
A tool used to tighten or loosen something.

Quiz Answers

1. Orville and Wilbur
2. True
3. Time Crunches
4. True
5. A propeller
6. A cuckoo
7. False—it was the *Wright Flyer*

DK | Penguin
Random
House

For my father and grandfather, pilots of the past.

Text for DK by Working Partners Ltd
9 Kingsway, London WC2B 6XF
With special thanks to Lucy Courtenay

Design by Collaborate Ltd
Illustrator Esther Hernando
Consultant Anita Ganeri
Acquisitions Editor James Mitchem
Editors Becca Arlington, Abi Maxwell
US Senior Editor Shannon Beatty
Designers Ann Cannings, Rachael Prokic, Elle Ward
Jacket and Sales Material Coordinator Magda Pszuk
Senior Production Editor Dragana Puvavic
Production Controller Leanne Burke
Publishing Director Sarah Larter

First American Edition, 2023
Published in the United States by DK Publishing
1745 Broadway, 20th Floor, New York, NY 10019
Text copyright © Working Partners Ltd 2023
Layout, illustration, and design copyright © 2023 Dorling
Kindersley Limited.

A Penguin Random House Company
23 24 25 26 27 10 9 8 7 6 5 4 3 2 1
001–327028–Sept/2023

Published in Great Britain by Dorling Kindersley Limited
A catalog record for this bookis available from the Library of Congress.
ISBN: 978-0-7440-6327-1 (Paperback)
ISBN: 978-0-7440-6329-5 (Hardcover)

DK books are available at special discounts when purchased in bulk
for sales promotions, premiums, fund-raising, oreducational use.
For details, contact:
DK Publishing Special Markets,
1745 Broadway, 20th Floor, New York, NY 10019
SpecialSales@dk.com

Printed and bound in Great Britain by
Clays Ltd, Elcograf S.p.A.

For the curious
www.dk.com

MIX
Paper | Supporting
responsible forestry
FSC™ C018179

This book was made with Forest
Stewardship Council™ certified
paper – one small step in DK's
commitment to a sustainable future.
For more information go to
www.dk.com/our-green-pledge